# The
# MESSI...

## The Last Prophet

# 12 12 2021

# by James D. Richardson

outskirtspress
DENVER, COLORADO

The Messenger
The Last Prophet
All Rights Reserved.
Copyright © 2014 James D. Richardson
v3.0

Outskirts Press, Inc.
http://www.outskirtspress.com

ISBN: 978-1-4787-4220-3

Outskirts Press and the "OP" logo are trademarks belonging to Outskirts Press, Inc.

PRINTED IN THE UNITED STATES OF AMERICA

*I dedicate this book to my sister Wendy Richardson. She took many prescribed pills over the years as an aid to get through life. She was trying to forget the horrible things she endured as a young child by our father. In short, Wendy passed away trying to forget her past. She did not die from an overdose. The pills finally caught up with her and her heart failed while she slept. In my heart I know she is one of God's angels now. I am so proud of her fight for life. Thank you, God, for looking out for her! I miss her deeply...*

# Contents

*The Messenger The Last Prophet* is a fiction story inspired by true events. All names were changed to protect the innocent. The story is about a boy that was asked by God at a young age to deliver a message to the world.

God said, "James Martin, I need you. I know you're only five years old but you are a special boy. I need you to deliver a message to the world for me. I would like it in the form of a book. I will send angels to look after you until you can complete your book with my message in it."

As a young boy James is afraid of his encounter with God and blocks it out, telling no one God had spoken to him at first. As he grows up, already coming from an abusive home, James endures many hardships and injuries while growing up. After many encounters and requests from God, James ignores him until God finally has enough.

God struck him with an illness and told James, "Now that I have your attention, I will heal you if you write the book! No more fooling around!"

James apologized and agreed. All healed up and at the age of 45, James encounters another visit from God to remind him of his calling and inform him of his message.

God said, "My angels have done a good job looking after you. You are well now. I think you put them to the test a few times too many. This message is important to me, James; this is why I spared your life. You and you alone are the messenger. You will deliver these words to all mankind in the form of a book so no man, woman, or child will ever forget. It's time men and women learn from their sins. Repair what I have created and prepare for the future. Our children are at risk and it's time to correct the issue."

James said, "God, I am sorry for ignoring you all of these years. I was confused and afraid and not sure where to start. I think I know where to start now and I will get started immediately!"

God said, "Thank you, James; do the best you can to deliver my words. I look forward to seeing what you come up with."

James said, "Thank you again for sparing my life. I will deliver your message…"

## Chapter One

# If You Could
# Only Imagine

I was at the age of four when we lived in a small town called Reed City. My parents had bought a large home just inside the city limits. My father was a short-fused-tempered man that seemed so unhappy most of the time. That year, he was in a motorcycle accident that almost cost him his life. We went to go see him at the hospital. When we walked in the room, he was barely alive. I looked at him lying there in the hospital bed with a large cast on his leg. It went from his toes all the way up to his hip. He was unconscious and was not aware that we were there. I was afraid for him because I loved him so much. He was my father and I missed him deeply. I reached up and held his hand; it was life-less. That accident changed him forever. I never told anyone until now, but I think he sold his soul to the devil to stay alive.

When my father came home from the hospital, he became this evil person and never looked back. His eyes were dark and he began to yell and scream at us a lot. Finally he began to enjoy beating us kids for no reason other than for pleasure, it seemed. I began to shut down and ignore him and shut out the world. My mother did very little to protect us. When the police came they did nothing either. They would speak to my father, but he would tell them we were making up stories. He pretended to be this injured man with a cane, and in no way could hurt a fly.

The police had bought his story and lectured us children and my mother for making up stories, and filing a false police report. That night we all got a good beating.

When it was my turn I yelled, "Dad, please stop! Please!"

I begged and pleaded with him some more to stop but I passed out from the beating. The next day when I awoke he was gone. I was in so much pain. We all licked our wounds and acted as if nothing ever happened. Some of our cuts should have been stitched up, but my mom was afraid of retaliation.

She said, "It's just best to let it go, you will be fine."

I have scars on my body for the rest of my life from that beating. We found out shortly after that incident that my father was having an affair with other women and did not come home much. This was a good thing since my real father died in the hospital. Since Dad was gone, so was our family's income. We starved for a few days until my mother found work. The neighbors all helped out with groceries from time to time while my father was gone. After a few months of roughing it, my father returned home and patched up things with my mother. We all tried to get along with our father the best we could, but things quickly returned to what most folks would call a nightmare. My father began beating us all over again and was molesting my older sisters. I overheard them talk about it and became sick to my stomach. It was wrong. I was curious and did not know what molesting was, so I asked my sister. She never said a word and began to cry as she looked at me. I stared into her eyes. They were full of fear. My heart went out to her.

Finally she said, "James, it's a secret, okay."

She held her finger to her tear-covered lips and whispered, "Shhhh!"

She began to blow her tears at me and a few of them hit my face. As they ran down my cheek, my eyes glazed over and filled with tears.

I whispered, "Okay, I'm sorry."

She whispered, "It's not your fault."

I whispered, "Okay, I'm still sorry."

She gave me a hug and sent me to my room. After many complaints to my mom from her, my mother did nothing to help her. On Sunday we went to our new church for some help with food but kept the molesting and the beatings a secret. My father conveniently missed our faces and hands so no one would see. Finally, my sister changed her mind about asking for help with my dad touching her. She was afraid but went for help anyways. We sat there that day listening to the priest talk about a man named Jesus, and how he was beaten and put on a cross to die. My heart went out to him because we had something in common. I stood up and spoke my mind. The priest had made me very angry at his story. We looked at each other eye to eye and then he nodded to me. No one else spoke a word but they sure did stare. I can't put my finger on it, but something in my heart changed that day.

Just after I turned five years old I had a dream. In my dream a man was talking to me about the future and how we were going to turn this world around and make it a better place together. The man made me feel warm and safe like no harm could come to me.

The man said, "James Martin, I need you. I know you're only five years old, but you are a special boy. I need you to deliver a message to the world for me. I would like it in the form of a book. I will send angels to look after you until you can complete your book with my message in it."

I said, "I am too little to do this."

The man said, "James, you are a strong boy. You will survive this."

I said, "Can you help my father? He is hurting my

sisters and brothers and me."

The man said, "It's too late for him now. I will look after you, though, and try and give your family some peace."

I said, "I am afraid."

The man said, "Do not fear me, because I am your creator. God is my name."

God made me feel strong, almost invincible. He took all of my fears away.

God said, "I will send angels to look over you, James."

I said, "What are angels?"

God said, "Angels do my work for me when I am occupied or busy with other serious matters."

I said, "What do they look like? How will I know?"

God said, "Angels come in many forms. You will know in your heart when they are around. Have the courage to listen to it. Focus on the book, James. The message must be powerful."

I said, "I don't know where to start?"

God said, "Learn about life first and then it will come to you. Don't forget how special you are."

I woke up the next morning confused and a little afraid; I was hungry too. I got up excited and want-ed to tell my older brother about my dream. Just as I went to say something to him, this feeling inside of me said, "Keep it to yourself." So I did. It was as if someone whispered in my ear. The hairs on my neck tingled or tickled a little.

The year before my father brought home a German shepherd puppy. We named him Shane. Shane became my best friend. He always growled at my father when he was near. His growls were mysterious. I never understood that until I got older. He looked at me with his big brown eyes all of the time. One day I was hungry so I went downstairs to the breezeway where we kept Shane's food. I sat down and began to eat with him. He cried out a little and licked my face. I felt as if he was telling me things would be okay. Either way, the dog food was not too bad, I thought. So I ate a few more pieces with him. Shane was my best friend and he followed me everywhere. From time to time, I would tie him to my Big Wheel and have him pull me around the block. One time we were going so fast! All I could see was his big feet and legs and his fluffy tail! Dirt was hitting me in the face as we raced down the sidewalk! I had my eyes squinted tight; they were almost closed.

I yelled, "Please stop, Shane! Please!"

I finally got my feet back on the pedals and held them tight! The front wheel skidded as Shane kept running! I turned my Big Wheel's handlebars sideways and it did not seem to help at all! Shane kept running! We seemed to pick up speed as we raced down the sidewalk! The back of the Big Wheel started to sway back and forth, skidding off the sidewalk and hitting the neighbor's grass and concrete steps! Pop! There went the back of my seat! Shane continued to run at full speed!

I yelled out, "We're going back for that!"

But Shane continued to run!

I yelled at the top of my lungs, "Shannne... stopppppp!"

All of a sudden we came to a stop. Shane was wagging his tail. I could feel the air from it, he was so close. I looked up and there was my older brother Jason looking down at me.

He said, "Why are you out here? I told you never to hook Shane up to the Big Wheel without me here!"

I said, "I know but I wanted to ride!"

Jason unhooked the rope that was tied around my Big Wheel and unhooked it from Shane. Shane turned around and licked the crap out of me.

I said, "Okay, I forgive you!"

I stood up and started pushing my Big Wheel home. It had a huge flat spot on the wheel from skidding for so long! It thumped when it rolled.

Jason said, "I told you that it was going to happen."

I looked up at him and he shook his head at me and smiled. He rubbed the top of my head and we went home. When it was my first day of kindergarten, my brother took me to school.

It was just after recess when one of my classmates said, "There is a puppy outside, Mrs. Linden."

The whole class walked to the window. I liked puppies too so I walked over to the window to look and there was Shane. I thought, how did he get off of his chain? I cracked the window more and Shane walked up to the glass. I stuck my arm out the window and he licked my hand.

I said, "You better get home, Shane. Get going before trouble comes."

He sat there looking at me. He turned his head sideways like he was confused and cried out…The kids all laughed at him.

Mrs. Linden said, "All right, class, that's enough. James, you can get your dog after school is over."

I smiled at him and went to sit in my seat. When school let out, there Shane was waiting for me. He ran up to me and gave me a great greeting—many licks on the face and head. My hair was soaked with drool. My brother had finally come and we began walking home.

My brother said, "When did Shane get here?"

I said, "I am not sure."

He rubbed his ears and we started walking home.

I said, "Shane, why didn't you go home when I said?"

He cried out at me and licked my hand.

My brother said, "Shane's lucky the police did not

come and take him away!"

I looked over at Shane and said, "No police!"

Shane whined some more and let out a deep bark! When we got back to the house, I had a good talk with Shane and told him to stay home from now on. He did not listen very well. We could never figure out how he broke the chain to get loose. Over the next six months my father finally had put him on a tow chain. No matter how big the chain was Shane always managed to get loose like it was magic. I would turn around and he would be right there looking at me.

We moved to Brighton that year. Things there only had gotten worse. Shane had to sleep outside in a dog-house. My father was having multiple affairs with the neighbors' wives. He was mad all of the time. We all walked on eggshells around him and my mother. My father had built a shed on our side yard. He was always out there fooling around with the neighbor women.

My mother said to me one day, "Lunch is ready, go tell your father."

I said, "Okay."

I walked outside to the shed. I slowly opened the door and had seen my father molesting my older sister. She was practically naked and crying and did not say a word to me. My father's pants were around his ankles. His eyes were dark and full of hate. I instantly began to weep at the sight of it.

My father yelled, "Shut the door, you little son of a bitch," in this deep and dark voice. I didn't—I ran inside the house and told my mother what was happening.

I yelled, "Mom, Dad is doing things to Shannon with his thingy."

My mother did nothing!

She said to me, "Quit making up stories and go and stand in the corner with your arms up!"

I walked over to the corner and stood there.

I said, "I swear, Mom, he is doing it, go look! His pants are down to the ground!"

My mom screamed, "Put your arms up!"

I went to put them up before she hit me. *Whack!* It was too late. She had hit me across the neck and face with a wet washcloth.

My mom said, "Kids, where do they come up with these stories?"

I could faintly hear her begin to cry. I felt horrible that she did not believe me. I also felt horrible I was too small to do anything about it. I cried some more but mostly on the inside. I was not sure at the time what was happening to my sisters, but I knew it was not good. That night before bed I said I was sorry to her.

She cried and gave me a hug and said, "Do not worry, Dad did not mean it, I forgive him, go on to bed, James."

A few days later the state police came to the house because of a complaint from the school nurse. They wanted to talk with my mom and dad. They believed what my dad had to say *again*. Just before they walked out, I approached the policeman. I remember asking him to please help my sister.

"Please Mr.... help her!" I said.

I had tears coming down my face and the look of desperation. My heart was screaming for their help!

The policemen looked at me and said, "It looks like we are all set here," to his partner and they left.

My dad beat me again for speaking out. I went to bed but could not sleep from the pain. I hurt everywhere. Blood soiled my pillow from a small cut to the side of my head. I felt so badly for my sisters and brothers. I did all I could to help them. That night I had another dream with God. I yelled at him for letting that happen to my sisters and brothers.

He said, "James, you don't understand. Give it time."

Time, I thought.

I said, "What do you mean? How could you let that happen, he is hurting her! Hurting us!"

I began to cry. I woke up crying my eyes out.

My brother woke up and said, "You better quiet down before you know who wakes up."

I said, "I don't care."

Truth was I really did not want to be beaten again.

I was so mad I decided to block God out for a while. I figured if God was so all and mighty, why is he letting these things happen to us?

When I was around six years old I was given a bike as a gift from my grandma. I loved it! I rode that bike everywhere, like around the block mostly. One day I was riding down the sidewalk and my neighbor's puppy ran in front of me. I turned to avoid hitting him and decided to cross the street. I turned and rode down the grass and went in between two parked cars. Then I was struck by a gold-colored Ford Falcon car. *BAM!* The car had sent me flying across the road and onto my neighbor's lawn. His tires began to squeal and the car came to a halt. At the point of impact on the grass, I rolled across the lawn and stood up on my own power without a scratch on me. I swear I must have flown 20 feet.

The neighbor lady screamed at the top of her lungs, "ARE YOU OKAY?"

I did not answer her. I nodded yes. People began to gather around after hearing the tire's squealing and metal crunching. I stood there in shock as the gentleman driving the car slowly got out and looked under his bumper.

He yelled, "Where did the little boy go?"

People began looking for me under the car. Another man opened up his hood searching for me. He was thinking I might have slid up into the engine compartment. I stood there absolutely crushed that my bike was mangled under the car. I turned to look at the gentleman driving the Falcon and he turned pale white right in front of my eyes. He walked over to the curb and sat down shaking and sweating. He kept leaning forward looking under the car for me.

He yelled again, "Where did he go?"

He began to cry. I slowly walked over to the man.

He yelled out again to the crowd of people, "Where did the little boy go?"

No one said a word. I continued to walk up to him. He had tears running down his face and the look of complete fear.

I said, "I am right here."

He looked up at me and said, "That's your bike?"

I said, "Yes, sir."

The man began to take deep breaths and started to get some color back in his face after a few minutes.

He looked up at me and said, "Don't you know not to ride in between two parked cars like that?"

I said calmly, "No, sir."

He barely could stand up, his knees were shaking so badly.

He said, "Kid, you are one lucky little shit! I should put you over my knee and teach you a thing or two about riding in the street."

My neighbor spoke up and said, "If you lay a finger

on that boy, I will teach you a thing or two about parenthood and driving slowly in a neighborhood!"

My neighbor said, "James, are you okay?"

I said, "Yes, sir."

He said, "Are you hurt?"

I said, "No, sir."

He rubbed the top of my head and said, "You are one lucky boy."

The man driving the car said, "Kid, I think God was watching out for you."

I quickly looked at him and stared.

The man said, "Hell, he must have sent angels to protect you or something."

I stood there looking at my bike and did not say anything back. Who would believe me anyway? I thought. The state police came with an ambulance right behind them. The trooper asked me what had happened. I stood there looking at the man that hit me. He still had the look of fear. I don't know why but I felt obligated to help him.

I said, "Trooper, this was my fault, I should have been looking for cars like my brother had taught me."

The trooper said, "Okay, son."

They looked me over and realized I did not have a scratch on me. I remember the look in the trooper's eyes. He looked amazed but confused.

He said, "You are very fortunate, son."

I smiled and said, "Can I go home now? I live right there," and pointed at my house across the street.

The police trooper said, "Go ahead and walk home."

I did. I walked as fast as I could. I had got inside the house and watched through the front window. A tow truck came and lifted the car up and removed my bike from underneath it. It was mangled. I began to cry. Don't get confused here. I was not crying about the bike. I was crying because I was so happy to be alive. I could not believe what had just happened to me. That car should have killed me, I thought. I looked around for angels and never saw anyone. No one had wings like in the Bible. I remember thinking, what do angels look like? Am I ever going to see one? Then I thought, why am I looking for something I don't know what it looks like? I shrugged my shoulders like it was no big deal and went to tell my mom what had just happened. I dried my tears on my t-shirt as I approached her. My mom was on the phone talking when I interrupted her.

I said, "Mom, I was hit by a car."

My mom said, "Shit I have to go!"

She hung up the phone and looked at me. I appeared to be fine to her.

She said, "Are you hurt?"

I said, "No, I am okay. The police are still outside."

She stood up and we looked out the window

together. The police let the man that hit me go and the tow truck took my bike away. The trooper soon left as well.

My mom said, "Oh James, that bike was brand new!"

I said, "I know, I am sorry."

My mom said, "I am glad you are okay."

She gave me a hug. That was the end of that. She never said a word to my father. After a little time all was forgotten until now. The next year I was playing on a hill with my little brother. We were rolling 6-inch to 10-inch rocks down a hill playing with G.I. Joes. We were causing these avalanches to happen with the large rocks. The rocks and dirt rolling down the hill would clobber our men at the bottom. We finally ran out of rocks so I told my brother I would be back and started to walk down the hill. I brought up a couple of the little rocks and went back down for more. While on my way down the hill, my brother rolled a couple of rocks down. One of the rocks hit me on the top of my head and knocked me down the hill the rest of the way. Blood began to ooze down my face and my neck and all over my dirty white t-shirt. My head was throbbing and I thought I was going to die.

I yelled, "Come on, Mike!"

I grabbed my bike and rode home as fast as I could. When I got to the house the blood had covered my whole shirt. My mom had seen me coming through the window and went into a panic and rushed outside to meet me. Mike finally caught up and went inside the house to sit with my older brother.

We did not have a car of our own, so my neighbor took us to the emergency room. My mom held a towel over the wound until we got there. The doctor quickly shaved my head and put several stitches in it. They took X-rays once they got the bleeding under control. I had a mild concussion and was lucky to be alive, the doctor said.

Doc said, "James, how did this happen to you?"

Something inside of me wanted to say my father did it, but it was not the truth. I told him the story about the rocks and G.I. Joes.

He looked at my mom and said these famous words: "Boys will be boys."

My mom seemed relieved that I was okay. She cried a lot. My head hurt so badly but I was glad to be alive. After hours of observation they finally sent us home. Later that night I thought I would get a nice lecture from my father about it. It was the opposite; he seemed to be careless to what had happened to me. I knew then he was an evil person. What made me mad was I could not do anything about it.

As other events took place, the police would not listen to my brothers or sisters or me. I was disappointed in them and lost respect for the law altogether. I did feel like a cat with nine lives, though. The doc told me how lucky I was again when we went back for the follow-up appointment. He reminded me to stay out of trouble.

I smiled and said, "I will try, Doc."

About six months later my older brother and I were arguing about something silly. He had shoved me a few times and punched me a couple of times as well. It made me mad that he could beat me up whenever he wanted and I could do nothing about it unless I told our mom. This particular day I went into the living room and said, "Mom, Jason is picking on me again."

It made my mom mad when the older kids picked on the little ones for some reason. It taught me then that as humans we pick our battles.

Mom yelled, "Get out here!"

Jason came out and sat on the couch while Mom lectured him and grounded him. Jason was mad. He picked up an apple and threw it at me as hard as he could. I was looking in the other direction when he threw it at me. His leg hit the table as he launched it at me. I turned to look at the noise. *Whack!* The apple had hit me in the nose, shattering my nose bone. Blood splattered everywhere. Back in the car we went to the hospital.

Jason kept saying "how sorry he was."

When we arrived back at the hospital the doctor had a sense of humor at least.

He said, "Back so soon, huh?"

I did not say a word. My mom was so mad, I swear steam was coming from her ears.

The doc smiled and said, "Let's have a look!"

I lay there thinking to myself, how many chances at life does someone get? Am I near the end? My faith in God returned. After all, something was keeping me alive. After the X-rays came back, the apple had broken my nose in three spots. The doctor finished cauterizing the wound to stop the bleeding. He then packed my nasal cavity with gauze bandages to keep the bones in place while they healed. I watched as he began to pack it in. It was in a roll package. All I can tell is…you can stuff a lot up there. I did not know just how much. I was amazed it took the whole package and a little from the next package to fill it.

The doctor said, "James, you are one lucky little boy. I think you have angels watching over you."

I looked at him closely for a moment and then he winked at me and then smiled.

I looked around, confused a little, and said "Thank you" to them.

I did not see anyone, but I think I knew what angels

were now. My sister explained it to me in church once after the bike accident. It did not click in my mind then. My brother was grounded for a while. He got a good whooping too. I had to go back weekly to get my nose repacked until it healed. After I healed up, I tried to avoid trouble as much as possible.

Chapter Two

# As I Grew Up

My parents had decided to get a divorce. When my mom told us kids the news, I was not surprised. I was glad to see him go because he was so mean. I must say I was proud of my mom for standing up for herself and us finally. I love her so much! See, Mom, I told the world! Besides living with Grandma now, I knew we would not starve all of the time. To me there is not a worse pain than hunger pains. Oh yes, Shane was allowed to come too! We moved from Brighton and in with my grandma for a while. She lived in Livonia, Michigan, on Angling Street.

The home was an all-fieldstone home my grandfather had built. It was beautiful and had an awesome fireplace inside. At the time, it was a great neighborhood. There was a community swimming pool and lots of trails to ride our bikes. Her two-acre backyard was mostly grass with a river at the end of her property. There were maple and pear trees and blueberry bushes on the property all over. The fence in the front was white and it stretched all the way across the front yard. There was a turnaround drive filled with small stones.

The home reminded me of a property you would see in England.

My family was a wild bunch. My older brother had turned 16 a while back and now had his license to drive. He was always in trouble with something. One day during the summer there, Jason had bought a Chrysler Newport. This car had a 440 four-barrel engine and was sassy.

Jason was bored and looking for excitement. He got the idea to take Grandpa's old wheelbarrow apart and use the tub to hook up to the back of his car.

He said, "Come on, it would be fun. I will go slowly."

I believed him. What a fool I was...

He punctured a hole in the tub and secured it with a tow chain. My uncle was there and had brought out a red, white, and blue helmet for me to wear and gave me his teardrop glasses. I looked over at Mike and Shane and smiled.

Jason said, "Are you afraid?"

I said, "Yes, wouldn't Evel Knievel be afraid?"

Yes! So I thought. Evel was my hero way back then, just for the record. I wanted to be just like him. I was off to a good start. I had two trips to the hospital E.R. on my belt. Anyway, after careful planning we began our first test run. I felt like a real stuntman sitting in that old wheelbarrow tub, with my teardrop shades and the "Spirit of '76" helmet. I put my hands on the sides of the tub and began to rock it from side to side. It felt solid to me and safe. Jason started the car. Reality set in quick. I was going to be towed by a car!

As quick as I had that thought and changed my mind, Jason punched it! I was getting pelted with the rocks, dirt, and grass that came from the rear tires. The rocks, dirt, and grass filled the barrow quickly. I could hear the engine rev and my brother's evil laugh! Ha, Ha, Ha, Ha, Ha, Ha!!! Jason turned the wheel and *zoom*, I was gone! I flew around the car at what felt like a hundred miles an hour and flew off the barrow, rolling onto the grass. I came skidding to a halt on my back.

I lay there waiting for pain to start but it did not come. I slowly stood up and looked up the yard. There they all stood: my uncle, Jason, and Mike, laughing. Shane stared at me. What a family, I thought.

Jason said, "You all right?"

I looked myself over real good. All I had was grass stains everywhere, including my arms and hands.

I said, "Yes."

He said, "Do you want to go again?"

I said, "Does anyone want to take a turn?"

They all said "No" at the same time. I stood there looking at them thinking to myself, they're missing out on life!

I yelled, "This moment will never be here again."

My uncle yelled back, "You are one weird kid!"

I said, "Okay, take it easy this time!"

Jason said, "I will."

My uncle yelled, "Hold on a minute," and walked into the house. He came out with a couple of pillows and a belt and tied them around my waist.

He said, "There, that should be safe."

I was cool with it in case I went sliding again. What I did not know was they were the pillows from my grandma's bed. Jason started the car and took off like a rocket! Shane began to bark! I was getting pelted all over again. It sure was fun, though! He turned the car and away I went! Wahoo! It was awesome! The wind had caught the helmet and pulled it back. The strap caught my chin and kept the helmet from coming off all the way. The force was so strong, it took all I had to stay on this time. I couldn't believe I was hanging on. He took off and got up some speed and turned the wheel again. *Swoosh!* Away I went again! It flung me around as fast as the first time. I hung on this time, though—again!

Mike yelled, "Look at the sparks!"

Jason got up some more speed and turned the wheel, sending me flying to my death; so I thought at the time. I flew off sliding across the grass, going straight towards the big maple tree. *Whack!* I hit the tree with my back and fell to my side. I lay there for a minute. They all came running. They asked me if I was okay. I slowly sat up and wiped the tears of joy from my face and said, "Yes, that was awesome!"

Shane began to lick my face and tugged at my helmet strap. I think he was trying to take it off for me.

"You guys have to try it! It's just an incredible feeling to be launched like that!" I said.

Jason said, "Fun's over."

He pointed at the barrow. It was folded in half and a large hole had been punched through the bottom. We all wondered how it bent like that.

All sad that the fun was over, I headed towards the house with the pillows, helmet, and sunglasses. I opened the screen door and I could hear my grandma say, "Where and the hell are my pillows?"

I freaked out and slid down the wall by the door and hid from her sight. I waited and listened for Grandma to leave her room. I heard her walk up into the living room so I stood up. I peeked around the door and ran the pillows to her room as fast as I could run. I tossed them onto her bed all dirty with grass stains and dirt. I am sure there was a hole or two in them as well. I looked again for her and ran outside.

As I hit the door I yelled, "Grandma knows about the pillows!"

We scattered! Mike and I were scared to death. Jason and my uncle laughed their butts off until tears slid down their faces.

I said, "How could you guys do that to Grandma?"

My uncle said, "Don't worry about it. She will be fine."

I felt bad for my grandma. She always looked out for us. That night my uncle got an earful from Grandma; this was not my uncle's first time taking her pillows, according to her. It was funny watching him get a good lecture for a change. My uncle was a spoiled little stinker. Weeks later we had to come up with other forms of excitement.

My uncle said, "There is a river behind the brush in the backyard. There is a trail in the corner of the property. Follow it down the steep hill and you will run right into it. We used to ice skate back there years ago."

We checked it out. We all stood there at the top of the hill and all I could think about was jumping it.

After a few minutes I said, "Let's jump it!"

Jason said, "Grandma has a wagon."

I said, "So? Let's jump it with bikes first."

Jason said, "We better not. You heard Mom if they get broken again. 'No more bikes,' she said, remember?"

I said, "Alright fine."

Jason came up with the idea to take the wagon down the hill and try and jump the river. I was listening! We all walked down there to check it out some more. My brother and uncle brought down an old wood door to use as a ramp. I stood on top of the hill looking down thinking. Is this what Evel felt like before he jumped Snake River? I was pumped! I stood there thinking; I felt like I'd used four of my nine lives up. I'd better slow down after this last stunt attempt. What's the worst that could happen? Get wet is all I could come up with. I decided to take the wagon halfway down the hill and launch it from there instead. My little brother Mike wanted to try the jump with me. I agreed and we climbed into the wagon together. My uncle and brother were watching closely.

My leg was the parking brake. I lifted my leg up and *zoom*—away we went! I tucked in my leg as we gained speed. The wheels were squeaking and the wagon was shaking! The wagon began to pick up more speed!

I said, "Thank God those angels are looking after me!"

My brother yelled, "What angels! I changed my mind, what angels?"

I said, "It's too late!"

*Bam!* We hit the ramp, launching the wagon high into the air! It felt like time had stopped. We had gotten some serious hang time! We came down right in the middle of the river on our backs... *Splash!* I let go of the handle and immediately stood up. I reached down and helped my brother up out of the water. He gasped for air as he came out! The water was not too deep there, just a couple of feet, but the current was fast. It was hard for us to stand up. We both stood there soaking wet and amazed because it was awesome to jump that high.

Jason yelled, "At least six feet high."

My uncle said, "That was awesome! Man, you guys are brave little shits!"

We both looked at him and said, "That was fun, let's go again!"

Jason said, "According to my precise calcula-tions…this time you need to do it from the top of the hill if you want to make it to the other side."

We stood there soaking wet, looking up at the steep hill. The hill from the bottom looking up seemed huge.

My uncle pulled the wagon to the top already and said, "Come on, what are you waiting for?"

Mike and I were looking up the hill assessing this carefully. Our teeth chattered a little as we slowly walked. Both of our bodies were shaking from the cold water. I thought I was just excited from adrenalin but it really was the cold water.

Jason said, "Come on, I will help you."

He grabbed our arms and helped us up the hill.

When we got up to the top I said, "It's time to rest and catch our breath first before we go."

After a few minutes' rest in the sun, we sat in the

wagon and got ready to go down. My uncle and older brother slid down the hill and sat by the river's edge to watch.

Mike said, "I am glad the river is not deep there."

I said, "Me too."

Mike said, "James, don't you ever get scared?"

I said, "Yes, all of the time."

Mike said, "Don't you ever worry about something bad happening to you?"

I said, "Yes, but I don't want to miss out on the moment. We may never get a chance to do this again."

Mike said, "I know everyone thinks you're weird, but I think you are the bravest boy I know. Please don't die on me."

I said, "Thank you, Mike, and let's get going. We are not going to die…just get wet a little. Let's show those dorks we are not afraid of this."

Without a word said Mike tucked his feet in and I slowly lifted my feet up, aiming us at the door ramp. *Swoosh!* Away we went! We were going so fast! All of a sudden something did not feel right. As we flew down the hill, I knew we were not going to make it across the river. The wagon handle began to shake, we were going so fast. The wagon almost slid out of control from fishtailing a little.

I yelled, "Lean back," to my brother.

He ignored me. I braced my feet on the edge of

the wagon and I pulled Mike back just as we hit the ramp—*Bam!* We hit the ramp and the front wheels of the wagon dug into the soft sand! We went flying like we were catapulted into the air, high up and over the ramp! We came splashing down into the river together. *Splash!* I quickly grabbed Mike. When we stood up and turned around, my uncle and my brother were clapping at us.

My uncle said, "That was excellent... Whoo!"

Jason continued to clap and said, "Man, I wish we had a movie box thing! That was awesome!"

My little brother said, "That was intense, I won't do it again."

I said, "We aren't! Today anyways."

I put my arm around him and said, "I think we are lucky that we did not hit the ramp."

We climbed out of the river and walked up to the top of the hill. We hung out in the backyard until we dried off. We were soaking wet. At times the wind would blow hard. We stood up when the breezes came. It helped to dry us off. We sat in the tall grass talking about the jump. Jason had brought up the wagon and it appeared to be okay. They left and went up to the house while Mike and I stayed to talk. I lay there wanting to share my dreams with him. Instead I asked my little brother if he believed in God.

He said, "I think so."

I said, "I do. I think God has been looking out for us."

Mike said, "What do you mean?"

I said, "Well take the last wagon jump. The wagon was going so fast I lost control of the handle. Someone straightened it out and had kept us on course."

Mike said, "That was not you?"

I said, "No, it wasn't."

Mike said, "Then who was it?"

I said, "I don't know for sure, God I guess."

Mike said, "What does God look like?"

I sat there for a minute and thought. I thought about my dreams and what God had said to me. I did not know what he looked like?

I said, "I am not sure."

I sat there a minute.

I said, "Has anyone ever talked to you in your sleep or your dreams?"

Mike said, "Yes, Santa Claus."

I said, "Anyone else?"

Mike said, "No, just Santa Claus."

I said, "Did Santa make you feel safe and comfortable?"

Mike said, "No, he told me I was a bad boy and I was not getting any gifts this year."

I could not help laughing.

I said, "Okay, Mike, for the record, you are not a bad boy."

Mike said, "Thank you."

He smiled at me and then gave me a hug. I sat there for a while thinking, I hope I am not losing my mind. It has been a while since God has spoken to me. Maybe he has given up on me since I got mad at him.

That year Shane had died and things seemed to get worse at my grandma's. I missed my best friend so much. Life was awkward and unstable with him gone. With Shane dying it taught me that none of us will be here forever. Mom had had enough with bad luck and seemed determined to change it on her own. To me, *evil* seemed to follow us wherever we went. I was so confused about life and what God had asked me to do. It did not take long and we had moved to West Bloomfield. My grandma had met a new man and wanted to sell her home right away, so my mom had rented a house off of Lochaven Road for us all. When we arrived at the house for the first time, there were shotgun shells all over the place. It looked like a war had taken place there. As I walked into the house, there were trails of blood stained into the hardwood floor. My mom tried to clean up most of it before we saw it.

She said, "It was pretty bad."

I asked her what had happened here.

She said, "The owner said a drug dealer rented the house and the police found out and raided it. A gunfight had broken out and the police had captured the man. That is all the owner said."

That was no big deal to me. We had been through a lot worse with my father. I shrugged my shoulders and followed my little brother in the house to our room. About a month had passed and I received another visit from God.

God said, "James, I see you are doing better."

I said, "I am."

God said, "I see your sisters are doing better as well."

I said, "They are doing well."

God said, "I think it's time we began our talk."

I said, "God, I am sorry for getting mad."

God said, "James, it is okay to be angry."

God also reassured me my father wouldn't hurt us anymore. I thanked him for that.

I said, "What did you do with him?"

God said, "Let's just say I put him with a woman that deserves him, okay?"

He went on about life and the importance of balance. God warned of the downfall of mankind if we did not change our ways.

God said, "Greed must be controlled, and wealth must be equal amongst the majority of the people."

He explained how important it was for leaders to maintain this balance. That man has begun to damage the balance again.

God said, "James, it must be preserved. Men who are given the ability, have the responsibility! In a few decades the largest automakers and insurance companies in the world will fall because of greed. Let's hope they learn from it."

Everything God had to say to me was confusing at the time.

I said, "I don't understand?"

God said, "Research what I explained to you. Do not share this information with anyone until the time is right. I will let you know when."

I said, "Alright, God. Can I ask you something?"

God said, "Please do."

I said, "Shane died so young…I just want to know why?"

God said, "James, dogs like Shane have a short lifespan. Enjoy them while you can. Do you see life is a journey?"

I said, "I do. I just miss my best friend."

God said, "Record what you feel and put it in the book."

I said, "Alright…I will start taking notes."

After what seemed like an eternity, I woke up feeling at peace with myself. I did not see God's face. He had the voice of a man, though. Although I missed Shane, my heart did not hurt as bad.

The next day we were out in the yard looking

for something to do. My uncle had a couple of old Mustangs he'd brought with him when he moved in with us. One was a six-cylinder automatic. The other was a 289 V8 three-speed. I sat in the driver's seat of the automatic car. I loved it!

I said to my uncle, "I can't wait to drive it!"

My uncle said, "You need to grow a little more. You're still a little guy."

I could not see over the dashboard. I sat in it listing to Honey Radio AM 56. It was so cool. I spent a lot of time in it that summer. My uncle would keep the battery charged for me so I could listen to the radio.

A few months later my uncle said, "Come on, I have an idea."

He took some straw bales apart and made me a booster seat for the Mustang. He took blocks of wood and fastened them to the brake and gas pedals.

He looked at me and said, "Are you ready?"

I said, "For what?"

He said, "To take a ride."

I said, "Me, drive? Yes I am ready!"

So I thought I was. My brother was a good teacher. I paid attention to everything he did so I could learn as much as possible.

My uncle climbed into the car and said, "Come on already."

I was so excited I forgot how to open the door. I

finally climbed into the driver's seat. I had seen the modifications my uncle had made for me.

I said, "You did that for me?"

He said, "I did. Before I give you the keys you need to listen to me. First thing is go slow so you can get a feel for it. It might be a six-cylinder car, but it still has a lot of power."

I said, "Okay."

My uncle said, "Second thing is the brake. When I say stop, you stop."

I said, "Okay."

He handed me the keys. I slowly inserted them into the ignition, feeling the tumblers click. I turned it over and *vroom!* It was running! My heart began to race with excitement like no other time! I put on the brake and slowly grabbed the gear shifter. I pushed in the release button and pulled it back into the drive gear. *Click, Click, Click!* I felt the transmission engage the rear tires. I was so pumped…all of this power at my control!

My uncle said, "Slowly now."

I said, "Okay!"

I let off the brake and slowly gave it some gas. I looked around the large twenty-acre field. I thought at least I wouldn't hit anything. I began to drive! Not only was I driving… I was driving a Mustang, baby! Whoooo! I slowly made turns and braked when my uncle said to stop.

I said, "This is so awesome, Uncle. Thank you for this!"

He smiled and said, "You are welcome."

As we cruised in the straw field I turned on the AM radio. I was having the time of my life! I couldn't wait to be sixteen and get my license.

My uncle said, "Have you ever done a doughnut?"

I said, "No, but I watched Jason do one with me behind him in a wheelbarrow!"

My uncle started laughing.

He said, "My brother told me about it."

I said, "It was pretty cool."

My uncle said, "You are one crazy kid!"

I said, "I am not crazy, it really was fun!"

He laughed some more.

He said, "All right, cut the wheel and give it all the gas you can."

I looked around first to make sure no one was coming and I punched it! Straw and dirt went flying everywhere as the car spun around in circles. It was awesome until this happened. As I was coming around a small hill there was a two-track road going to the back of the property. The rear tire hit the groove of the track and tipped the Mustang up on its side. My uncle quickly turned the car off.

He said, "Holy shit, I did not see that coming! At

least we had our seatbelts on, huh!"

I sat there looking down at my uncle, scared. He must have seen the fear in my eyes and said, "Don't worry, the car is okay."

I said, "Okay, I am sorry!"

He said, "James, it is okay... don't worry."

I could feel the front tire still rolling.

He said, "You get out first, and then I will get out."

I slowly undid my seatbelt and fell on my uncle, laughing my butt off. He laughed too and helped me up. I climbed out of the car and jumped down to the ground. My uncle slowly climbed out and jumped down next to me.

He said, "Come on, we better walk back to the house and get help to flip it back on its wheels."

I said, "Okay."

We began our walk back. As we walked I said, "Have you ever seen God?"

My uncle said, "No, I have not."

I waited a minute and said, "Have you ever spoken with him?"

My uncle looked at me and said, "Well... I have asked him for a favor or two once. But I never heard anything back."

I waited a minute and said, "Uncle, if you don't mind me asking, what was it you wanted from God?"

My uncle looked at me and stopped walking. He

stared into my eyes and said, "I wished to have my *children* back!"

He began to weep. Not a full-blown breakdown, but tears were flowing down his face.

I said, "You do miss them, don't you."

He said, "I do, very much!"

I said, "Where did they end up?"

My uncle said, "They live in Florida by the gulf."

I realized then that my uncle was hurting badly.

He dried his eyes and said, "Please do not tell anyone about this, okay?"

I said, "Okay."

My cousins were taken away from my uncle in a divorce. My aunt moved south to torture him and it seemed to be working quite well. We walked back over the hill and up to the house. My older brother was back with my other uncle, and we told them what had happened to us. My brother put a tow chain in the trunk of his car and we all climbed into it. When we drove over the hill, my uncle and my brother began to laugh hysterically!

My Uncle Dean said, "Ha, ha, ha, real funny! Come on; let's get it flipped back on its wheels."

My brother backed up to the Mustang and parked the car. He got out the chain and hooked it around the rear axle of the Mustang.

My Uncle Dean said, "Come over here and push

with us."

I said, "Okay."

My brother got in his car and started it up. He slowly gave it gas and the Mustang fell back onto its wheels—effortlessly on our part. My brother unhooked the chain and began to stretch it out to tow the Mustang back to the house.

My Uncle Dean said, "Hold up for a second, let's see if she will start?"

He inserted the key and began to turn the engine over—*vroom*, it started.

My uncle said, "Come on, James, drive us home!"

I thought my driving days were all over. I ran to the car and climbed in.

My brother said, "Come on, I will race you!"

My uncle said, "Let him win this time, I don't know about you but I have had enough excitement for today."

I smiled and said, "Okay."

As we slowly drove back to the house my uncle said, "Thank you for listening to me and keeping my secret."

I said, "I wouldn't tell a soul. I promise!"

He said, "Thank you. Someday I will see them again before I die."

I don't know why, but at that very moment, I felt in my heart that he would see them again someday. Later that night we had a large bonfire. My uncle sat there all quiet and sad.

I sat next to him and said, "Thanks again for today. It was awesome! Even flipping the car on its side was exciting!"

My uncle smiled and said, "It was fun. Can I ask you something?"

I said, "Sure."

He said, "Have you spoken with God before?"

I sat there for a second and did not know what to say. I did not want to lie.

I said, "In my dreams, Uncle, a man comes to me. He makes me feel safe and warm like no harm is going to come to me. I cannot clearly see his face but I know it's him."

My uncle stared at me for a minute and then smiled and said, "Could you ask him a favor for me the next time you speak to him?"

I said, "Of course!"

My uncle said, "You remember our talk?"

I said, "Yes."

My uncle said, "Could you ask him to forgive me and send my children home someday?"

I shook my head yes and then said, "Yes, I will ask him."

After a few minutes my uncle said to me, "What does God want with a little boy, you think?"

I smiled and said, "For now, it's between me and God, okay?"

Without hesitation my uncle rubbed the top of my head and said, "Okay, don't forget to ask him."

I sat there looking into the flames watching the lumber burn. I began to fall asleep on everyone. I decided to go to bed.

I said, "Good night, you guys," and I walked into the house and climbed in bed.

As I lay there I thought back to the time when I last spoke with God. I was still confused about what exactly he wanted as far as a book goes. He also asked me to learn about secret codes so I could put his message in the form of one. I figured if anyone could read my writing, which was enough code in itself. I wondered who would take the time to decode a message; it was something to think about. In school I learned about Rome's political greed problems and what they did to people. God said they were a great nation once. I fell asleep thinking about him as well. Hours later God came to me in my sleep.

He said, "James, it has been a while since we have spoken. I see you are doing well."

I said, "I am. I was just talking about you today. I also have been having fun just like you say, you like your children best when they are at play."

God said, "I do! Have you been working on our project?"

I said, "I have. I have learned much about Rome's

downfall." We talked for a while about it.

God said, "Well, continue your education on the subject of greed and I will come and see you again soon."

I said, "Okay, God, could I ask a favor?"

He was silent for a moment.

I said, "God, are you there?"

God said, "James, I am here, what is the favor you ask of me?"

I said, "My uncle misses his children, and I wondered if you could help him soon? He wants to see them again."

God said, "Your uncle can be a selfish man, James. Selfish people get what they deserve here on earth."

I said, "I know, but he loves his kids."

God said, "I will handle the situation, but do not speak to him on my behalf."

I said, "Okay, I will not say a word to him even if he asks me again."

God said, "Continue your education like I asked of you. Remember what I said about the balance of life and the importance of it as well. Remember, James, you are only here one time on earth. Make the best of it."

I lay there thinking about what God had said.

I said, "God, I told my uncle I have spoken to you. I did not tell him about what you asked of me, but I did not want to lie when he asked me."

God said, "Very good, James. It's okay to say you speak to me."

I said, "Okay."

I felt a lot better knowing he did not mind.

I said, "God, I also wanted to say I know I have taken a lot of risks with my life. I sure do love the thrills and excitement that life has to offer."

God said, "You are learning the balance quickly. Keep learning, James. Remember to have fun but not too much fun."

I woke up the next morning and got up to go find something to eat. I walked into the kitchen and could not believe the mess. My uncles had drunk all of the beer and had eaten the entire loaf of bread and package of bologna. I opened the fridge and it was empty as well. My stomach roared with hunger. It made me mad those guys ate all of the bread and bologna. I thought it was selfish of them, like God had said.

I sat down at the kitchen table thinking about what God said last night. I repeated, "You are only here once, make the best of it," in my mind. I thought to myself, I couldn't be the only one who knows this? I really did not know much about heaven and the afterworld. I did not even know if there was such a thing. If I only could remember to ask, I had a couple of questions for God, but I always seemed to forget to ask them. I got dressed and walked outside. I looked over where the campfire was, and there were my uncles and my brother sleeping on the ground. I walked over to them and began to laugh. All of them had mustard smeared on their faces. It looked like they'd had a good time. All the anger I had inside of me suddenly disappeared. My only thought was, I hoped God would help my uncle. I believe everybody deserves a second chance. We are only human after all. I sure was learning from my mistakes.

That summer seemed to pass by fast. School had begun; I started the sixth grade at a school called Four Towns Elementary. A couple times a week, the teacher would take us to the library to read for a couple of hours. The other children there treated me different. What I mean by different is, they did not seem to pick on me like they did the other new students. Most were extremely nice. All of the girls were very nice to me as well. I made friends quickly. A boy named Paul Arlington and a girl named Rosemarie Bennett became my good friends. Sixth-grade camp was approaching quickly and that's all that seemed to be on our minds. I did not forget about God or what he wanted me to do. It was going to take time for me to put things in perspective anyway.

# Chapter Three
# The Tenth Attempt

Our school was not very big and our library was not very big either. I read what I could about Rome and its downfall. I researched other civilizations as well. In short, they all had the same thing in common: Greed and power-hungry men seemed to be their downfall. At this point, I was nowhere close or did I have the ability to write down on paper to complete God's message. I lay there in bed thinking how I could begin this book and deliver a message that every man, woman, and child could understand. I felt it was important that they knew of the journey I took to get this to them as well. I decided that was going to be my starting point. I clearly needed more information and decided to put things on hold for a while and try to live my life the best I could. I still could not figure out why God chose me. Why me? I'm nobody special, I thought. There are a lot of great men and women that are far more intelligent than I. Men that had already written great novels and delivered them throughout the world. Talk about pressure!

The next day on the playground I was sitting on the

merry-go-round with Paul and Rosemarie. Rosemarie could tell something was wrong with me.

She asked, "James, why do you seem so distant?"

I said, "I am okay."

But really I was afraid to tell anyone about my dreams about God and him talking to me. I did not think anyone would understand. I liked my new friends and did not want to scare them away. I could only imagine them looking at me like I was a freak if I told them. Rosemarie was persistent and kept asking me what was bothering me. I told her she would not understand and that I was confused about my problem as well.

Rosemarie said, "I think that you need to speak to the school counselor."

I sat there for a moment considering her advice. I smiled at Rosemarie and lied.

I said, "It's my father, he is an abusive person."

Rosemarie put her hand on my shoulder and said, "See, that was not so bad now, was it?"

She walked away. I felt like total crap for lying but I knew in my heart she would not understand the truth. We are talking about God here. Not some priest at a church. No offence, fellas!

A few minutes later Paul walked up to me and said, "I was sorry about your father being abusive."

At that very moment I realized I did not lie to them

after all. My father was abusive. I just didn't tell them about God. I guess some things happen for a reason. Maybe this was what God meant when he said I would understand later? I quickly changed the subject. Paul and I talked about camp and how much fun we were going to have. Paul had heard that they were going to let us shoot rifles. Paul was excited because they had a 12-gauge shotgun to shoot. The rest of the afternoon, he went on and on like he was some big game hunter going on safari. Paul was a silly boy with big dreams. He was a smart boy that liked to laugh too. Paul was the kind of friend that when you thought about him, he would make you smile. I wish I had more friends like that.

A week before camp we went on a field trip to the public library. It was only for a couple of hours so I had to make my time count. I searched for books about life and death and secret codes. Rosemarie clung to me like glue. She was watching what I was choosing to read. Every time I reached for a book, she looked at me concerned. I felt as if I was running out of time if I did not get more research done.

Rosemarie said, "Why are you looking at those books about spirits?"

I said, "Aren't you curious where we go when you die?"

Rosemarie sat there with a confused look on her

face and said, "No, I am going to heaven to see my grandmother and be with her."

I said, "How do you know you're going there?"

Rosemarie pushed me and I fell backwards into the bookshelf.

I quickly said, "That was unnecessary!"

Rosemarie said, "I am sorry, James! We all go to heaven!"

I said, "Okay, Rosemarie, calm down."

Rosemarie said, "My mother says there is no hell and it's a sin to talk about it. So don't bring it up again, and quit reading those books!"

I decided not to argue with her, especially at the library. I did throw her a curveball though and walked over to the encyclopedia section and took out two that had the letter S on the bottom. I carried the books over to Rosemarie's table and sat down next to her. Rosemarie did not pay any attention to my books and kept reading hers. I'd begun to search through my books when Paul came over and sat down on the other side of me and whispered, "Check this out!"

Paul had got *The Guinness Book of World Records*. I did not know at the time they had books like this. Paul immediately opened it to the longest jump section. There he was, the man himself: Evel Knievel. I stood up and walked over to take a peek at the book Paul had.

The two hours went by fast; our teacher yelled

out, "Let's go! Please return your books back to their proper place."

"Make sure they make it back to their proper place," she said again.

I thought to myself, holy smokes, I just ruined my chance for research again and I got so caught up with the Guinness book. Our teacher yelled out "Quickly now" as she stared at her watch. I walked up to the teacher and asked if I could check out these two encyclopedia books.

In a deep and dark voice the teacher said, "NO, James, you cannot!"

Then she smiled at me. Her teeth were black and pointed almost like a sharpened pencil.

She growled and said, "Put them away and get in line!"

It was a growl you would never forget. I looked up at her and her eyes were dark black with dark black veins on her face and neck. She startled me a little. I did not hesitate; I did as she asked and returned them to their proper place and stood in line. Rosemarie was already in line when she looked back at me.

She walked back to where I was and said, "I can't believe she would not let you take those out."

I pretended nothing had happened and said, "I don't understand either."

I thought no one seemed to notice the teacher's

change. I thought to myself, what in God's name was that all about? When we got back to the classroom I sat in my chair looking forward, and I was keeping to myself. The teacher sat down at her desk and stared at me with those black eyes. We looked at each other eye to eye and I remembered what God had said to me once.

God said there would be people that will do everything they can to stop you from succeeding in your journey. "You must learn to overcome and adapt," he said. "James, you must learn to fly by the seat of your pants to beat them."

I stared back at the teacher directly into her eyes until she turned away. I continued to stare at her. On occasion she would look back at me and stare at me for a moment. The bell had rung and everyone got up quickly and began to walk out of the class.

The teacher said as I passed by and in the same dark voice, "Will I be seeing you tomorrow, James?"

With confidence I said, "Oh yes."

I continued to walk out of the room.

When I caught up to Rosemarie and Paul, Rosemarie said, "That was the weirdest thing I've ever heard our teacher say."

I tried to just blow it off like I did not hear anything.

Rosemarie tugged on my shirt and said, "Did you hear me?"

I said, "I'm sorry, Rosemarie, were you speaking

to me?"

She said, "Yes, I heard what the teacher had said to you! I think the teacher is weird."

I said, "Yes, she is a little strange," and left it at that.

When we got outside I looked up at the classroom window and the teacher was staring through the glass looking at me. Rosemarie turned to see what I was looking at and noticed the teacher looking down at us.

Rosemarie grabbed my arm and said, "Just ignore her! That creepy old witch! What a freak!"

I walked with Paul and Rosemarie to the bus.

I said, "I will see you guys tomorrow."

Rosemarie smiled and walked on the bus.

Paul said, "See you tomorrow!"

I walked to the end of the bus line and turned around and looked up at the school. My teacher was still staring in my direction. For some reason I did not feel creeped out or afraid of her. I walked across Cooley Lake Road to catch up to my little brother Mike. I turned around to look one last time. There she was still staring! The busses all pulled out.

As we were walking home I could hear Rosemarie yell at the top of her lungs, "See you tomorrow," out of the window! Lord, that girl had some lungs! I pegged her to be a gym teacher for sure when she grew up.

My brother Mike says, "The girl wants to marry you."

I said, "You're crazy! You don't know what you're talking about."

Mike said, "I'm just saying what I heard at school. The rumor is Rosemarie wants to marry you."

I said, "We're just friends, it's not like that."

Mike began to sing, "Rosemarie and James sitting in a tree! KISSING! First comes..."

I shoved him into a bush to shut him up.

Mike stood up and said, "Okay, I will be quiet."

The next morning we were walking to school and everything seemed to be normal. Mike and I walked across the road and into the school. Rosemarie and Paul were waiting there for me.

Rosemarie said, "Did you see her yet?"

I said, "No, why?"

Rosemarie said, "I just wondered."

I said, "You and Paul go first, I will walk behind you, Rosemarie."

Mike began to giggle. I pushed him into the boy's bathroom as we passed by to get rid of him. A couple of other boys were right behind Mike, making it difficult for him to get out.

Mike made it out finally and yelled, "That's not funny! I'm telling Mom!"

I stuck my tongue out at him and gave him a raspberry as I walked up the steps. As I approached the classroom, I hid behind Rosemarie as we passed the teacher's desk. I sat down in my seat and acted like nothing ever happened. The teacher was writing our assignment on the chalkboard with her back to us. I glanced over at Rosemarie and Paul. Rosemarie shrugged her shoulders like it was no big deal.

The teacher turned around and said, "Good morning, class."

We all said good morning to her. Everything seemed to be okay and normal again. After yesterday I did not know what to expect. It sure was weird.

Over the next few weeks' things seemed to be somewhat normal. I began preparing for camp. I had to borrow a sleeping bag and a duffel bag from my uncle. He loaned me the ones the Army issued him. Getting my clothes together for seven days was not difficult at all. I only owned three pairs of pants and four shirts, five pairs of underwear, and six pairs of socks. As I finished packing I thought to myself, that was easy. I couldn't understand why my Rosemarie was making such a big deal about packing. The next day I figured it out. It was time for camp. When I got to school I met up with Rosemarie while she was standing in line for the bus. She had enough stuff to last her a month.

Rosemarie looked at me and said, "Where is your luggage?"

I threw down the Army duffel bag and said, "It's all in there."

Rosemarie said, "You're kidding me?"

I said, "Nope, this is how poor people travel."

Rosemarie looked down at my duffel bag and began to laugh. Her parents were wealthy and spoiled her with lots of clothing and many other items. I was happy for her. Rosemarie looked back at her fleet of luggage. I turned to look at her luggage and counted five suitcases and a travel bag she had around her shoulder. That totaled six pieces of luggage.

I said, "We are only going for a week?"

Rosemarie looked at me with tears in her eyes and said, "I'm sorry, I should not be making fun of your wealth."

I said, "Rosemarie, I know you're wealthy and I think that's great for you and your family. Being poor isn't so bad, besides I do not know what it's like to be wealthy. I just make do with what I have. Please don't cry or feel sorry for me. I am okay with it."

Rosemarie hugged me and said, "You're my best friend, James."

I hugged her back and said, "Please stop crying. You're my best friend too!"

Another student was behind us and said as he pushed us down on top of the luggage together, "Get a room!"

While I was standing up I said, "That was a big mistake, kid."

The kid said, "Yes, what are you going to do about it?"

I said, "It's not me you have to worry about."

As Rosemarie stood up she punched the kid right between the eyes, knocking him down onto the ground.

The rest of the students began to laugh at the boy.

I raised my eyebrows and said, "Nice one," as Rosemarie shook her hand back and forth.

Rosemarie said, "That hurt like hell."

She kicked the boy very hard in the back of the leg, causing him to squeal out loud.

Rosemarie yelled, "Nobody touches me!"

After a few minutes the boy stood up and said, "I'm going to tell the principal on you!"

Rosemarie said, "Go for it! Go on and tell the principal you got beat up by a girl."

The boy stopped in his tracks and turned around and stood there looking at Rosemarie and me.

I could not help but say, "I promise not to tell anyone."

The rest of our sixth-grade class began to laugh at him. We finally got on the bus and sat with Paul.

Paul said, "I had seen the whole thing through the window. That was awesome, Rosemarie!"

Rosemarie said, "Thank you."

She did not celebrate it much. She held her hand

and just kept to herself in the seat.

I heard her say, "What a dumb-ass," under her breath. I smiled at her.

When we got to camp they divided us up and showed us to our cabins. Each cabin held 18 students. Paul and I were split up as well. At first it was a big deal until we realized we weren't spending much time in the cabins. They were there to sleep in only. On the second day of camp the counselors had us pair up with the girls for an egg toss. Rosemarie was nowhere in sight. We talked at school how we would pair up no matter what. I could not find her.

I yelled out, "Rosemarie!"

She did not respond. After waiting for a few minutes the counselors yelled out again, "Find a partner quickly now!"

I looked over at Paul and he had found a girl from the West Bloomfield School District that came to camp with us. I gave him the thumbs-up as he smiled back at me and pointed behind me.

I turned around expecting Rosemarie, but found a beautiful blonde-haired girl instead.

She said, "James, right?"

I said, "Yes it is."

"Hi! I am Lisa and I go to West Bloomfield."

I said, "It's nice to meet you."

We shook hands.

Lisa asked, "Do you have a partner yet?"

I said, "No, not yet. How did you know my name?"

Lisa said, "Rosemarie told me."

I said, "Where is she?"

Lisa said, "Down the hill with my twin brother."

I did not know what to say at first. Then it came to me.

I said, "I would like to be your partner."

Lisa said, "Great!"

She stuck out her hand. I grabbed her hand and we walked to the egg-toss line close to Paul. Lisa and I stood there talking.

Lisa said, "Rosemarie is in my cabin, and we are bunk buddies."

I said, "That explains some of it."

Lisa said, "We were talking about cute guys and well, your name came up."

I smiled at Lisa and said, "Thank you."

After a few seconds I said, "You are pretty cute yourself."

Lisa said, "It was weird at first talking to Rosemarie. Rosemarie would not tell me what you looked like. She said just walk over the hill and you will know it's him. So I did; and when I got to the top of the hill, there you were. I just knew it was you. There is something special about you."

Lisa looked into my eyes.

I stared back at her and said, "We better get in line."

The counselor yelled out, "All right, if everyone would take five steps back!"

I continued to look into Lisa's eyes as I stepped backwards. At the time I thought they were this cool dark blue, tropical color.

As we began our egg toss, I had forgotten all about Rosemarie. Next to Rosemarie, Lisa was the prettiest girl at camp. After we lost and the egg toss was over, Lisa and I decided to take a walk down by the lake. When we got down to the lake, it was heavily wooded with small trails going through the woods. We walked the trails hand in hand, talking. We could hear giggling as we walked through the woods. When we approached a couple under a jacket Lisa said, "Ben... is that you?"

The jacket slowly rose up and their Ben was with Rosemarie.

Lisa says, "Ben, this is James."

I said, "Hello, Ben. Hello, Rosemarie!"

I was a little frustrated with Rosemarie at the time. Lisa helped me take my mind off of her quickly. She never let go of my hand.

Lisa said, "We are going for a walk."

I stuck my tongue out at Rosemarie as Lisa pulled me away.

Rosemarie smiled and said, "I'll talk to you guys later on."

They pulled the jacket back over their heads and began making out. Lisa and I walked further up the trail to where the beach was. We took our shoes off and sat close to the edge of the water. Lisa did not waste any time. As soon as I sat down she leaned in for a kiss. Now at this point in my life I had never kissed a girl before. Well my mom on the cheek and Grandma on the cheek…that's it. I slowly leaned the rest of the way and touched her lips with mine. Her lips were so soft and smooth. It was beautiful, I thought. We pulled apart for a brief moment and looked into each other's eyes. The only thought in my mind was to kiss her again. I slowly leaned in towards her until my lips met hers for a second time. At that very moment I thought I was the luckiest kid in the world. Wow!

It seemed like hours had passed in seconds and it was time for dinner. All I knew was that if love was that powerful, I was looking for more! The dinner bell was ringing. We stood up and cleaned off each other's bottoms. Lisa asked if I was going to the dance later.

I said I was and that I would see her there.

I reached for her hand and said, "Come on, let's get through dinner first."

Lisa smiled and grabbed my hand. We walked back up to the mess hall for dinner. The girls were supposed to eat in the east dining hall and the boys in the west. Lisa and I agreed to grab our plates and met back up outside at the picnic table. When I stood in line all I could think about was Lisa. She was beautiful and smart and beautiful and had gorgeous eyes…and she kisses well. I looked through the windows for her while I waited in line. Other kids had to tell me to move up several times. Towards the end of the food line I took what I had and left for the bread table. I grabbed two rolls and two butters and walked outside to watch for her. When I came out there was Lisa waiting for me. Our eyes reconnected and we slowly walked towards each other. Once together we kissed again in front of everyone. Someone had let out a whistle or two. We held hands as we walked to the tables. When we got out there Rosemarie and Ben had the same idea.

Lisa whispered, "Come on, let's get our own table."

We walked over to the furthest picnic table away and sat down. Lisa began to ask me questions about Rosemarie. I told her how cool Rosemarie was and how fun she is to be around.

I said, "She packs a nice right hand if you know what I mean."

Lisa said, "Really, I did not expect her to be that type."

I said, "She's not, but when she's provoked or touched inappropriately she is."

Lisa said, "Enough about Rosemarie, what about you? What does James like?"

I said, "I like thrills, like roller coasters, fast cars, and stunts and beautiful girls named Lisa."

Lisa giggled a little and looked into my eyes and said, "I can see that in you. What stunts have you done?"

I told her about the time when my brother and I tried to jump the river twice behind my Grandma's. Lisa was laughing so hard she fell off the picnic table and landed on her butt. She continued to laugh as she stood up and cleaned herself off. I didn't see the humor in it. Maybe it was the way I said it? I went on and on about my injuries and the time we rolled the Mustang. She felt the knot on my head and felt bad for me. I told her a little about my parents.

I said, "What about you? What's the beautiful Lisa like in this big world?"

Lisa said, "I have great parents and a brother who you met briefly. I like school and look forward to going to Yale where my mom went. She is an attorney in Southfield. Her and my dad is like night and day. My dad is a graduate from the community college and works in communication. They met at a mutual friend's party and hit it off like us!"

I smiled at her and kissed her again.

I said, "What else…what do you want to be when you grow up?"

Lisa smiled and said, "A great mommy once I graduate from college. I want to be an attorney like my mom and my grandma. I think what they do is awesome and inspiring helping others solve their differences. As far as personal things I like computers, horseback riding, and camping of course. I like softball and basketball. I like having goals and I look forward to buying a beautiful home and filling it with memories."

I said, "That's a pretty mature response. Sounds like you have it all planned out. That's awesome."

Lisa said, "What do you want to be when you grow up besides stunts?"

I said, "Well… I have some big goals. I would like to be an author someday. Maybe write a fiction book or an occasional science fiction novel?"

Lisa giggled a little and said, "That would be so cool."

Lisa and I had a great week and probably the best time together that any sixth-grade camp kid could have. We did everything together from the egg toss to saying good-bye at the bus. What a kiss good-bye we gave each other. That girl made me smile and laugh so hard quite a few times, especially when she wanted to try and shoot the twelve-gauge shotgun. I tried to talk her out of it, but she insisted. When she pulled the trigger it knocked her right on her butt! She dropped the gun on the ground.

The instructor quickly helped her up and, "That's not supposed to happen!"

I stood there asking if she was okay. She began to

laugh and I laughed with her. The whole camp had heard about it by dinnertime. As I climbed onto the bus and waved good-bye to her, she blew me a kiss. I smiled and sat in my seat. Paul slid in the seat next to me and we both closed our eyes, exhausted.

That night after washing my whole wardrobe, I finished folding my clothes and stored them away in my dresser. After a long week it was time to go to bed.

As fast as I went to sleep I could hear God say, "James, how are you?"

I said, "I am well. I had a great time at camp and met some great people there."

God said, "How is the research going?"

I said, "Not so well. I messed up my trip to the library. My friend Paul showed me a book that had all of these world records in it. I had to see some of them. It totally distracted me from reading the encyclopedias."

God was quiet.

I said, "God, something strange happened to me a few weeks ago. My teacher was acting strangely when I asked her to check out a few books."

God said, "Oh?"

I said, "When we returned to class, she stared at me like she wanted me dead or something. Her eyes were black and her teeth were pointed. Her skin looked pale as if she were dead."

God said, "Maybe they are on to us already. I'd

hoped the move would slow them down. Which books did you want to check out?"

I said, "The ones that contained spiritual content. I wanted to know more about heaven. What happens to us when we die?"

God said, "James, every human has a spirit. It's what makes us each unique. In due time you will learn more… I need you to focus on learning the balance of life. There is much to be done."

I said, "Okay. You know that teacher; the other part that was strange is she watched me walk home that day and never moved. I kept looking back to see if she had left but she was still there. Who is on to us?"

God was silent for a moment.

God said, "This is the tenth attempt they have made to kill you or frighten you into quitting your journey."

I remained quiet.

God said, "James, are you afraid of Lucifer?"

I sat there a minute and thought hard; I knew very little about who he was.

I said, "No! I am not! He has not harmed me yet and I will not quit until the book is finished. The angels you have sent are doing a great job looking after me."

God said, "James, you will need to remain fearless while on your journey. Tell no one about the book. It now is a secret until you can complete it. Do you understand me?"

I said, "Yes, God, I do."

God said, "I will handle the teacher. You go to school as if nothing happened and tell no one of this."

I said, "Okay."

God said, "James, I am proud of you. You are my chosen one. Do the best you can to continue your research."

I said, "I do not get very many opportunities to go to the library. My mother is always too tired to take me."

God said, "James, just do the best you can! Good night, James."

I said, "Good night."

It was the first time God had said "good night" to me. He usually just goes.

The following Monday I was at school a little early to see if the teacher came to school. I did not see her. Rosemarie and Paul were in the hallway waiting for me as usual when I peeked around the staircase. I whistled and they both turned around.

Rosemarie said, "What are you doing up there already?"

I said, "Come on, you guys!"

I couldn't tell them anything.

Paul said, "What are you doing here so early?"

I said, "My watch was off is all."

Paul bought it.

Rosemarie looked down at my wrist and saw that

I did not wear a watch. I looked her in the eyes and shook my head back and forth for her not to say a word. I motioned with my mouth, "I will explain later." Rosemarie smiled and nodded okay. We sat in class as the rest of the students came in. Our teacher Mrs. Kerker did not show up.

The principal had come into the room and said, "Mrs. Kerker has fallen seriously ill and will not be here for the week."

I think my jaw had hit the desktop, I could not believe my own ears. I was thinking God kicked her ass for messing with me! I wanted to yell out and celebrate the news but I couldn't.

The principal continued, "You have a substitute teacher coming named Ms. Washington. She will be here momentarily. Please be on your best behavior for her and show her respect."

The principal walked out of the room. At the click of the door closing, the class went crazy with papers flying everywhere. I looked over at Paul and he was participating in the paper toss. Not Rosemarie though. She stared at me with her gorgeous blue, curious eyes.

She said calmly, "What do you know about this?"

I said, "Nothing, how could I?"

Rosemarie said, "I don't know why, but I have a strange feeling you do."

I said, "Rosemarie, come on, be real here!"

I quickly changed the subject to Ben.

I said, "How is Ben doing?"

Rosemarie said, "He dumped me for another girl. That pig!"

I said, "I am sorry to hear that. I know you liked him."

Rosemarie said, "You are so sweet, James. I don't want to share you with anyone ever again. That Lisa is mean too. Are you going to see her again soon?"

I said, "Rosemarie, we are just friends. That's it!"

Rosemarie smiled and said, "Meet me on the playground by the slide in the back," and she raised her eyebrows at me.

I smiled and slid back into my chair. Ms. Washington came walking into the room and stood at the door. The class went silent.

She slowly shut the door and calmly said, "Please pick up the papers on the floor and put them in the trash."

Everyone sat there quietly staring at her.

She snapped out a "right now!!!"

The class moved as fast as they could—Ms. Washington meant business.

She said, "Pass these out!"

She handed a stack of papers to each student in the front of the rows of chairs.

As they were being handed back she said,

"Wednesday we are going on a field trip to the public library."

I quickly looked up at her. She was not looking at me, though. I was handed my permission slip. I could not believe my own eyes and ears! I thought to myself, God is Awesome!

Rosemarie whispered, "Do not screw this up this time."

I quickly turned to look at her.

Ms. Washington said, "We are checking books out on this trip."

I looked back over at Rosemarie. She looked me in the eyes and winked at me. I thought, does she know? How could she? There is no way…

## Chapter Four

# Ramp to Ramp

Just after the library trip, my mom announced we were moving again. I could not understand why. I was angry with her. She explained that her job relocated her to the Livingston County branch, and we were moving to Howell, Michigan.

She yelled, "Pack up!"

I spent a whole two hours packing this time. I did not have much as it was. I read as much as I could before I had to take back the books. I spent as much time as I could watching the world news and the local coverage as well. I went to school the next day all depressed about the news about moving. When I walked into the school, there were Rosemarie and Paul waiting for me.

I said, "I need to tell you guys something."

Rosemarie acted as if she already knew and began to cry. She hugged me so tight I could barely breathe.

She said, "I am going to miss you. It's not every day you get a best friend."

I said, "I am going to miss you too…I can barely breathe, Rosemarie. Let me go."

Wow that girl was strong for a little frame. She let go a little bit and kissed me long and firm! It was that kind of kiss you never forget. Everyone in the school was watching, including the principal. She walked over and separated us again.

She said, "The other day out on the playground was enough, I said! This is a school, young lady, a place of education—not a make-out spot!"

Rosemarie went to say something when the principal cut her off.

She said, "Shhhh; NOT A WORRDD! James… go to class!"

I stood there ignoring her. I was waiting for Rosemarie to come with me.

The principal said, "Go now, James!"

She pointed up the stairs. I walked up the steps with Paul.

Paul said, "What happened on the playground?"

I said, "Well, Rosemarie said she wanted to talk with me. She had asked me to meet her out on the playground by the slide in the back. When I got out there she said she did not want to share me with any other women and kissed me like she meant it. While we were making out, the principal caught us while she was walking the perimeter fence. Man, was she pissed!"

Paul said, "Wow, Rosemarie really likes you a lot. You are lucky, James; she is the prettiest sixth-grader in Waterford… Maybe even the whole world!"

I said, "Thanks, Paul. Now, I have to say good-bye to her and you; I am moving."

Paul said, "You're shitting me!"

I said, "No, that's what I was trying to tell you both downstairs while Rosemarie was kissing me."

Paul gave me a hug and then shook my hand.

He said, "James, it's been my pleasure."

I said, "Me too, Paul. I hope to see you again someday."

Paul said, "When are you moving?"

I said, "This weekend."

Paul said, "Well, we have a couple days still, let's make the best of it. Where are you moving to?"

I said, "I guess to Howell."

Paul said, "Where is that?"

I held up my trusty map my right hand (it's a Michigan thing)—and pointed to Howell's whereabouts.

I said, "Right about there."

Paul said, "That's a long ways away, James. I won't be able to visit."

I could not help laughing at him.

I said, "It's okay. Hopefully when we get older we can look each other up."

Paul said, "Yeah that sounds perfect."

About a half hour later, Rosemarie came into class and sat in her seat next to me.

Rosemarie said, "Sorry, James, you're up next."

I said, "No big deal."

The principal called me out into the hallway. I stood up and winked at Rosemarie. She smiled and that was all that mattered to me. I smiled back and made my way to the door. As I approached her she had an evil look on her face. So evil, in fact, it reminded me of Aunt Ester on *Fred Sanford*. That lady scared me for some reason.

When I got there she said, "Rosemarie explained to me that you are moving soon?"

I said, "Yes, ma'am."

She said, "That's why she kissed you."

I said, "Yes ma'am!"

The principal looked up at Rosemarie and then back at me. I tried to not look at her.

She said, "I am sorry to hear the news, James. We were getting so close."

I said, "Me too, ma'am!"

She said in a very low and growling voice, "It was planned, you little shit."

I looked up at her and stared into her eyes. They turned black at that very moment. Her veins on her forehead turned as well. Then her skin turned pale!

She said in a very deep voice, "Go sit in your seat, I am not quite done with you yet…you little bastard… you will perish before you finish!"

I said in a calm but firm voice, "I am not afraid of you! I will triumph!"

Not another word was said. I stared at her for a moment and then walked back to my seat in the classroom and sat down. She stared at me through the glass in the door for a few minutes and then walked away. Rosemarie looked afraid and did not say a word to me until we got outside of the school.

As soon as we hit the sidewalk she said, "That principal is a freak too. Did you see her eyes? They were just like our teacher's."

I tried to ignore her statement.

I said, "Rosemarie, it will be okay I promise."

Rosemarie said, "Tell me you saw that witch? When are you moving?"

I said, "I did and I am going this weekend. I probably won't be here on Friday, though, knowing my mom's past behavior. She likes to be done by Saturday so she can rest on Sunday."

Rosemarie said, "Okay, I better go."

She kissed me and then turned and walked on the bus with Paul.

I said, "I will see you guys tomorrow."

I began to walk home. I crossed the street and caught up to my little brother.

As soon as I got close he said, "I was called down to the office today."

I said, "For what?"

Mike said, "They never said the reason why. All they wanted to know was where we were moving to."

I said, "Did you tell them?"

Mike said, "Yes; what was the big deal?"

I said, "Nothing, nothing at all... You actually said 'Howell'?"

Mike said, "Yes, are you deaf!"

I turned to look at the school and there was the principal, staring out of my classroom window. I turned back around and continued my way home with Mike. Every ten feet I kept looking back to see if she had left...she did not.

Mike said, "Why are you acting silly?"

I said, "I guess because we are moving and I am going to miss my friends."

Mike said, "Yeah me too, I guess. I hate moving so much. I feel like I don't have a home. Does it bother you, James?"

I said, "It does...but I found if you have God and Jesus in your heart home is where the heart is... if that makes any sense?"

Mike said, "I like God and Jesus. It's all really confusing to me."

I said, "As long as you are with family that's all that matters. We have each other. As you get older it will make more sense to you. If not just ask. I will be happy to explain it again."

Mike said, "I wish we had a dad. Why is he so mean, James?"

I said, "I cannot answer for him…I am not sure why Dad does what he does. It's confusing to me as well. Try to move on without him, Mikey… It's for the best."

Mike said, "What do you mean it's for the best?"

I said, "You know that kid at school that asked too many questions and gets beat on all of the time?"

Mike said, "Yes, why?"

I said, "Don't be that kid."

Mike said, "You said I can ask you!"

I said, "Mikey, take a break with the questions, al-right? I need rest too."

As we approached our long driveway, I could hear a car coming from behind us. It sounded like it was coming at a high rate of speed. At the last second I turned around to look at it and I ran and pushed Mike out of the way before the car struck us both. Mike fell into a mud puddle and began to cry. The car fishtailed back and forth as if it was going out of control!

He stood up and yelled, "What is wrong with you! I was going to wear these again tomorrow!"

I said, "Mike, I am sorry…didn't you see the car?"

Mike said, "What car?"

I said, "That grey one that almost ran us over?"

Mike said, "You mean that one?"

I looked up the road and the grey car had turned around and had stopped about ten houses down. They revved the engine a few times.

I said, "Yes, that one."

Scared, Mike started walking down the driveway as fast as he could. I stared at the grey car for a few minutes and it finally drove away. I could not tell who was driving.

I yelled, "Mikey, wait up!"

When I caught up to Mike I said, "Don't tell anyone about this, okay?"

Mike said, "No one will listen anyways."

I said, "I am always here to listen to you, Mike... always! Just keep it between me and you please."

Mike said, "Okay."

I said, "Mike, I am sorry I lost my patience with you back there. I think when you have problems you need to overcome them and adapt to the change. It will make life easier on you."

Mikey said, "What are you saying? You're weird, James."

I said, "Look at it this way. We are moving, right?"

Mike said, "Yes."

I said, "You don't like it right because we are changing homes again?"

Mike said, "Yeah."

I said, "Accept the change and adapt to it. You will get used to it like we did the last few moves."

Mike said, "You got issues, James, where do you come up with this stuff?"

I said, "Give it some thought, Mikey. It will make sense soon."

When we got back to the house I had seen that the washer and dryer were still hooked up. I told him to get his dirty clothes together and I washed Mike's clothes for him. I felt bad for pushing him down like that. Better than being run over, though! I felt bad for Mikey. Being little and not having someone listening to you really hurts bad...especially your parents... I knew exactly how he felt and I was always going to try and be here for him. That afternoon we made sandwiches for dinner and sat down to watch our little TV. No one else was home. My mom was working late and my uncles were busy moving stuff to the new house. They had taken a lot of our furniture already. It looked like we would be gone by Friday for sure. Later that evening when my mom came home, she thanked me for looking after Mikey. Mikey had fallen asleep on the couch and my mom carried him to his bed.

She stared into my eyes and said, "What is going on in that little mind of yours?"

I said, "I don't know where to start."

Mom said, "How was school...I called to let them

know of the transfer. That principal is a strange one."

I said, "You are right she is strange."

Mom said, "I know you have a hard time talking to me, James. I am trying to mend my wrongs here. Please give me a chance to...okay?"

At that moment I felt sorry for her. I tried to understand why she did what she did. I guess I wouldn't understand until I had kids of my own. Maybe I will never fully understand. That's life, I guess.

I said, "Mom, I have a lot on my plate and I am trying to do the best I can in school. Trouble seems to follow me wherever I go."

Mom said, "I heard about the kiss from your principal. Is Rosemarie your girlfriend?"

I said, "Mom, she is my best friend and I am going to miss her."

Mom said, "Get her address and you can write each other."

I said, "I have her address, Mom. Rosemarie does not want to write me. She just wants to move on and that is what hurts, okay? She is pissed that I am moving. Now you know. I am going to bed...good night."

My mom said, "There are other girls out there, James."

I did not say another word and walked into my bedroom and shut the door. I stared at my brother for a minute and put Mikey's covers up to his head and climbed into bed. I lay there thinking about Rosemarie and Paul and finally fell asleep. That night I felt like I had the weight of the world on my shoulders.

The next day we were walking to school. We walked into the parking lot when Mike said, "Isn't that the grey car from yesterday?"

I looked at it closely and said, "It is! It looks just the same!"

Where it was parked there was a faded sign in front of it. It read, "Principal Parking Only."

I said, "Don't say a word to anyone, Mike."

Mike said, "I won't now...why did she do that, James?"

I didn't know what to say...it just came out.

I said, "Maybe she's upset we're moving? I am not sure... just stay clear of her. Come and get me if you have to. Do you remember the emergency exit?"

Mike said, "I do remember."

I said, "Use it if you must."

When we walked inside, the principal was acting like a fool again as she usually did. I focused on her eyes. Her eye color was normal. Later that day the principal announced over the P.A. the death of Mrs. Kerker. She died peacefully in her sleep. I raised an eyebrow at the news. She also explained that Ms. Washington would be staying on as her replacement. Rosemarie seemed very distant all day Thursday. I kept trying to speak to her but she ignored my attempts. Paul seemed depressed too. I hoped they knew I was going to miss them both dearly. When the bell rang to go home I walked outside. I had seen Paul and Rosemarie waiting for me. When I got up to them, Rosemarie gave me a good-bye kiss to remember her by.

She said, "I will always remember you, James."

I said, "I will always remember you."

Just like that she walked onto the bus.

Paul said, "Good luck, buddy!"

I shook his hand and said, "Take care, Paul."

Paul walked onto the bus and sat down in front of Rosemarie. I waved good-bye to them both and turned away. I ran and caught up to my brother for the walk home. Mike did not say a word all the way home. I decided to let him be. When we got up to the house, my mom had the moving trailer packed and ready to go!

She said, "Take one last walkthrough, boys, and then get in the car with your uncle."

I walked through the house and back out the front door. We climbed into my uncle's car and drove away. I never looked back each time we moved. I thought about God's words: overcome and adapt! An hour and a half later we were pulling into the driveway of our new home. It was right next door to a funeral parlor.

I looked at my brother and said, "This is going to be interesting!"

Mike said, "No, it's not! It's going to be scary!"

I looked up at the old house on Crane Street. It was scary! It had a creepy, mysterious look. (Later on I found out it used to be the old funeral home.) I went to swallow, but my mouth was dry. I don't know what I was nervous about; the house did not do anything to me. As we entered the front entrance, the hair on my neck stood up. I felt as if I'd entered a new world of evil. I looked down at my little brother and he seemed terrified.

I said, "Do not let this old house scare you."

Mike said, "I'll try…are you scared?"

I lied through my teeth and said, "Oh no, no of course not. Come on, let's go upstairs and pick out a room. Mom said we get first pick."

The truth was I really was scared… this old house had my full attention. We slowly walked up the large staircase. Every step I took, the boards beneath my feet creaked. It made a very distinctive, eerie sound.

Mike said, "Talk about creepy!"

I said, "Just keep going."

About 20 minutes later we decided on the room that faced the school. It was not the largest one, but it was the least scary.

Mike said, "This room makes me feel safe."

I said, "Okay, this is it then."

We began to unpack our belongings. My uncles

brought up our dressers and put them in place for us. Jason came upstairs and looked over the last two rooms available. He chose the large room at the end of the hallway.

Jason yelled out, "Remember my rules! No one is allowed in my room!"

Mike yelled back, "Don't worry, you just picked the creepiest room in the whole house!"

My uncles overheard us talking and began to laugh at Mike's reply. He opened the door across from ours and turned on the light.

He said, "I guess this one is mine?"

He threw down his duffel bags and went back downstairs for more of his belongings. Mike and I made up our beds and finished fixing up our room.

Mike sat down on his bed and said, "Do you think we could stay in here for a while?"

I said, "I am hungry, let's go downstairs and get some food. Then we can come back up here for the night."

Mike agreed. We went downstairs and toured the rest of the large house. As I walked through I quickly came up with this reference. (This old house made the Adams family house look like a church… that's how scary it was.) This house had four large bedrooms, one large bathroom downstairs, and the bathroom upstairs in between my brother's room and my uncles'. The main level consisted of my mom's large room, living room, sitting room, large kitchen, dining room, and a large family room.

Mike and I made some bologna sandwiches and were watching my uncles move lumber from the large family room in the back of the house out to the garage.

One of my uncles came in the house and said, "It's too bad you don't have any bicycles. There's enough lumber there to make some nice ramps to jump from."

My Uncle Dean overheard my other uncle and said, "Well, we will have to remedy that, won't we!"

I smiled because I knew what my uncle meant. My Uncle Dean was a good man. He had helped our family a lot financially. We watched them finish moving the rest of the lumber out to the garage.

Uncle Dean said, "Let's get settled in here first, and then we will go to the Schwinn dealer at the beginning of the week and see what they have. Okay?"

Mike and I both smiled and said, "Okay."

That night I lay in bed thinking about my friends Rosemarie and Paul. I missed them a lot already. I hated moving around so much. Every time we moved, I felt I was leaving a part of my soul behind. Mike fell asleep right away. I could hear my uncle snoring and my brother talking to his girlfriend. He was trying to talk her into having sex. She had kept turning him down.

She said, "Stop it, Jason. Your little brothers will

hear us."

I laughed as he kept saying, "But baby, I need you. Come on…you know you want it too."

He said it over and over like a broken record. I finally dozed off and got some sleep.

The next morning my mom went to the local bakery with my uncles and brought back some donuts for breakfast. We all sat around the large table the former tenants had left behind. The table sat 10 people comfortably. When my brother Jason and his girlfriend came downstairs to eat, I could not help but say, "But baby, I need you."

Mike began to giggle because I told him what was going on last night. My mom shook her head back and forth and began to laugh at us making fun of Jason.

Mom asked, "How did everyone sleep?"

I said, "I slept well."

Mike said, "Pretty good, Mom."

Jason said, "We slept well."

Uncle Dean said, "Not too bad once Jason shut up."

We all laughed some more. Monday morning my mom took us to enroll us in school. Every time we moved we never knew what to expect being the new kids. The first day did not go so well for Mike. On his way home two kids about my size were picking on him. I ran to his aid as fast as I could. The boys were punching him in the head and in the stomach. My older brother Jason taught me well to defend myself but not to bully other people. He was a black belt in tae kwon do. (Personally I liked the street rules better because no rules applied.) As I approached I decided to attack! I ran up and threw an elbow into the face of the taller boy, knocking him down to the ground and causing his nose to bleed. I then turned to his friend, punching him in the throat, causing him to fend for himself. Poor Mike was lying on the ground crying and all beat up. His nose was bleeding and his face began to bruise.

It made me so angry that I turned around and kicked the larger boy in the groin! He cried out for help! I looked at the other boy. He was still gasping for air. Nobody else wanted to get involved. I picked Mike up off the ground and we headed home. He was beat up pretty badly. My mom cleaned him up and finally got his nose to quit bleeding. I sat there thinking I did not do enough to help him. I should have given them the same treatment. That night I did not say much and watched over Mikey like he was my own son.

The next day my mom was furious with the two boys and wanted something done about it. She went to the principal for help. When we arrived at the school, the two boys and their parents were already there claiming that they were the ones beaten up by us. The principal, after hearing our side, put two and two together and realized the other two boys were at fault. He apologized to my mother, Mike, and me. The father of the two boys looked at me like he was going to kill me.

In a low voice he looked at my mother and said, "This is not over yet!"

The principal said, "Yes it is!"

It wasn't, though...

The next day in class I made some new friends. A boy named William congratulated me for beating up the school bullies.

A girl named Leslie said, "That boy David has been harassing me for a long time. I am glad you are here, James."

I said, "You're welcome, but I really did not want to hurt anyone. The truth was, they were beating up my little brother, and I had no choice but to take action."

They felt bad for Mike. At lunchtime I sat with William and Leslie and a couple of her friends. David and a few of his football friends came over to our table. I looked up and saw the principal watching David's every move and remained calm.

David said, "You are sitting with my girlfriend, and I don't like it!"

Leslie said, "I am not your girlfriend, David, for the hundredth time!"

William said, "Maybe it's time you learn English, David!"

David said, "William, you have an ass-kicking coming!"

I said, "David, you like being a bully, don't you?"

David said, "At the end of the day, you'd be begging me to stop!"

I said, "Maybe I will, or maybe you will!"

David said, "I will be waiting for you after school! I'll see you soon," and he blew me a kiss.

I thought, what a weirdo. When school let out David didn't care who was watching or who was there. He walked over to William and punched him in the face, causing his nose to bleed.

He walked right up to me and shoved me and said, "Let's go," and began swinging at me.

One of his friends got down on the ground behind me as David went to push me, hoping I would fall to the ground. I leaned to the left as David charged me and he tripped over his friend.

Everyone began to laugh at him, including his friends. Leslie was close by, laughing at David. David stood up and shoved Leslie hard, causing her to fall to the ground. That seemed to be what it took to make me mad enough to do what I did. All in one motion I grabbed David's shirt with my left hand and grabbed his groin with my right, picking David up off the ground. I squeezed his groin hard. He began to cry out in pain as I turned him around. The garbage dumpster was right there with the lid already open. I walked him over to the edge of the garbage dumpster and let him go. He fell into the garbage bags crying.

At this point the principal had come over and said, "That's enough!"

He opened the dumpster and reached for David.

The principal yelled out, "The show's over, go home!"

The crowd began to thin out. I turned to walk away when the principal said, "James, I don't think so!"

William and Leslie stayed with me. The principal looked at me and said, "This is all done. I don't want you two fighting anymore. David, do you understand me?"

David said "Yes, sir" in a high-pitched voice.

William and Leslie began to laugh a little at David's new voice.

The principal turned and looked at the rest of David's friends and said, "I don't want to suspend any of you. But if you come to my office again with fighting issues, you will be suspended and permanently removed from the football team."

The rest of the boys said, "Yes, sir!"

The principal sent them all home.

He said, "Leslie and William, you go on home now, James and I need to have a little talk."

Leslie and William walked away.

The principal said, "I know it is hard being the new kid in school. I was the new kid several times growing up. So I understand what you're going through. But what I don't understand is why you have to provoke fights. Are you saying things to David?"

I said, "No, sir! I'm not provoking anything! I never said anything to that boy. He was the one that was beating up my little brother."

The principal said, "You're probably right. That David has been a lot of trouble here in the great city of Howell."

He stood there for a moment.

The principal said, "You go on home now, James, I'm sure your family is missing you."

I said, "Yes sir, see you tomorrow."

The principal said, "Very well," and turned around and walked away.

While I was walking home I hoped that was the end of it. As I walked around to the front of the building, William and Leslie were there waiting for me.

William said, "David wouldn't mess with you anymore. You just embarrassed the shit out of him."

I said, "Leslie, are you okay?"

Leslie said, "I am; just a little dirty."

I said, "William, you should go home and get yourself cleaned up. You have blood all the way down to your belt."

William looked down at himself and said, "I suppose you're right."

I said, "I better get going. I'll see you guys tomorrow."

When I got home my mom was waiting for me. I told her everything that had happened. My mom felt bad for me.

She said, "At least you are okay and not into trouble. I have a surprise for you!"

I said, "Really, what is it?"

She said, "Get in the car and I will show you."

I walked out to the car and climbed in. Mom came out and we began to drive away. We drove about 10 blocks and my mom stopped in front of the Howell Public Library.

I looked up at my mom and said, "This is awesome!" She says, "I know you like to read. This is one of the reasons why I chose this city. They have a very large library."

I gave my mom a hug and said, "Thank you."

We walked inside the library; my mom helped me sign up for my very own library card. At that very moment I thought my mom would mess her pants if she knew what I needed to do the research for, if she knew just how special her son really was. God's messenger!

Mom said, "Come on, your uncle is waiting for you!"

I had forgotten all about the bikes my uncle wanted to buy for us. We walked back out to the car and my mom drove us to the Schwinn dealer just outside of town. When we pulled in the parking lot, my uncle was there with my little brother. They were there waiting for us for over an hour. I was so excited!

Uncle Dean said, "Go with your brother and pick out a bike."

I said, "Any bike?"

Uncle Dean said, "Any bike you want!"

I walked as fast as I could inside the store. I looked back at my Uncle Dean and my mom. They both had a lot of happiness and joy in their facial expressions. I turned back to look at my brother and he had found a bike that he wanted. It was a cool BMX bike.

I wanted a new BMX bike as well but did not see the color I was after. The salesperson saw me wandering in the store and said, "Can I help you find something?"

I said, "Yes, I was looking for the newest BMX bike in red."

The salesman said, "I do not have any on the floor, but I do have a brand-new one in the box, it will need to be assembled. If you have a half an hour I can assemble it for you?"

I said, "Just a second, let me check with my uncle?"

I walked outside and said, "Uncle Dean, do we have time for him to assemble my new bike?"

Uncle Dean said, "Of course we do!"

My mom said, "I'm going to head home, Uncle

Dean will bring you home."

I said "Good-bye" to my mom and walked back inside the store.

I told the salesperson, "Okay, we will wait."

Just like he said, a half an hour later he was finished. My eyes lit up as he came around the counter with my new red bike. I sat on the bike and the salesman adjusted the seat and handlebars to fit me properly. I thanked my Uncle Dean again for the new bike. It was so cool! Uncle Dean loaded up the bikes in the trunk of his large Pontiac and we headed home.

Uncle Dean said, "I have one more surprise for you and your brother."

Mike said, "It's going to be sweet!"

I said, "Mike, you already know what it is?"

Mike said, "Yes, I helped build it. We did it while you were doing your homework upstairs."

I couldn't wait to get home. We got back to the house and unloaded the bikes.

Uncle Dean said, "Wait here and close your eyes. I'll tell you when you can open your eyes."

I said, "Okay."

I heard the garage door open and could hear Uncle Dean struggling and making these groaning sounds.

After what seemed like 5 minutes, Uncle Dean came up to me and said, "Follow me, but keep your eyes closed."

I grabbed ahold of Uncle Dean's belt loop and followed him to the front yard.

He said, "Okay, open your eyes!"

I opened my eyes and there was the coolest thing I had ever seen. My very own jumping ramps! Uncle Dean had built one to launch from and one to land on.

Uncle Dean said, "The ramps are eight feet long by three feet wide and three feet tall."

He was very excited. He explained how I could move them further apart as we got better. He pointed out that the sidewalks were 3 feet x 3 feet slabs of concrete.

"You will be able to measure how far you jump!"

Uncle Dean sat down on the steps and watched Mike and I attempt our first jump. I began peddling my bike and rode up the ramp slowly like Evel Knievel checking things out. I slowly rolled backwards and rode back to my starting point. I began peddling my bike and rode up the ramp and jumped through the air and landed on the landing ramp.

My uncle began to clap and said, "Okay, let's try it a little further apart than 2 inches."

I said, "Okay."

Mike rode up the ramp and barely came down the other side. He was so excited.

He said, "James, did you see me?"

I said, "I did!"

His bike never left the ramp, but I didn't have the heart to tell him.

Uncle Dean said, "Maybe for today you should just keep them close together so Mike will be safe. When he's not around you can make it whatever distance you feel safe."

I said, "Thank you again, Uncle Dean, you're the best!"

Uncle Dean smiled and said, "Be careful, I need to go and get dinner started. Mom has to work for a while."

Mike and I must've rode up and down the ramp a hundred times before my mom finally called us in for the night. There was something special about that ramp that made me forget all my troubles. It made me feel so free and alive. Over the next few weeks that's all I talked about. My friends from school and other kids in the neighborhood came around to watch and try the ramps. Things in the neighborhood seemed to settle down quickly and Mike and I were making more new friends. There were about fifteen kids in the neighborhood that loved the ramps. Every day about five o'clock they were coming over to help get the ramps out of the garage. When Mike was not around, we were putting the ramps almost three full concrete slabs apart. We estimated it around ten to twelve feet.

My new older friends were really cool when Mike

was around. We needed to keep the ramps close together for him and some of his friends to enjoy it as
well. Once in a while Mike would say, "Let's see who
can jump the furthest." Mike and his little buddies
would sit in the grass and watch as the ramps went
further and further apart. One of my school friends
soon became the "King of the Ramps."

As the weather became cooler it was no fun staying
outside in the cold. I began spending more time at the
library anyways. I researched a lot more of fallen civilizations and the balance of life. Leslie and William liked
to read as well. Occasionally they would join me at
the library. Leslie was always curious about the books I
would read and check out. One day she asked me what
I thought about heaven and if there is one.

I thought for a second and said, "I believe in my
heart there is one. Only special people get to go there,
though. You cannot commit a crime and expect to go
to heaven. I think God does forgive certain people that
make honest mistakes. I do believe if you take another
human's life, you would not go there. It's not in our
nature to kill man, woman, or child."

Leslie and William listened to me as I went on
about God and my beliefs.

I said, "Life is so precious and short. I think we are
only here one time, and we need to do the best we can
to make it to heaven. I don't think most people know

this. Or at least I think they forgot. There is a certain balance to life that must be respected at all times. The rich need to look after the poor and unable, but they do not. Not enough anyways."

Leslie said, "What is the balance of life you mentioned?"

I said, "I think one part of the balance of life is helping others to survive. If you have the ability to succeed better than most, you have the responsibility to look after mankind. Greed has been the downfall of many wonderful civilizations. Power-hungry men that did not want to share anything. They thought they could take the wealth with them when they died. How funny is that?"

Leslie said, "Pretty funny!"

I said, "There are many other topics to the balance of life that need attention like not using so much of our natural resources, helping third-world countries get control of their population. Educating them to do better, and the list goes on!"

I stopped because of my promise to God.

Leslie said, "That makes sense."

I said, "I am sorry, you guys, I did not mean to go on and on about it."

William said, "I think it's really cool you have a passion about it."

Leslie said, "Yes, it's cool."

I thought, if they only knew the truth.

William said, "It clearly makes sense what you're saying."

I said, "Thank you, William."

I thought, one down and 5 billion to go! This was not going to be an easy task! I continued to read about the power of sharing and its rewards. It was very inspiring and educational. But it was missing a few key ingredients. As the evening closed I said good-bye to William and Leslie and headed home with my books.

While I was riding home, I thought about God and the balance of life some more. I was disappointed in what I had learned so far and what I had seen with my own eyes. I wondered what these greedy men thought when they were hording all of the planet's money. They were going to take it with them… I began to laugh out loud. Now that's funny, I thought. I thought about the cycle of life. You are young when you start out with barely anything. You get a job and then a home. You begin to raise a family. In the Bible God clearly states, "go forth and multiply." You raise your kids the best you can and teach them to be productive citizens of the world.

You then retire, trying to survive, and then soon death comes. What I had seen so far in my youth is that your belongings and cash you worked so hard for are then divided amongst your children, unless they fight. Then the government steps in and wants their share of the tax money. By the time the lawyers and court system are done with the funds, they split up the remaining balance amongst the surviving children that are now not speaking to each other because of greed. They barely get any of their father's hard-earned cash that he saved for them in the first place. This is ugly! It needs to be repaired. This is not a quality way of life God intended for us. Has anyone read the **Declaration of Independence** lately? I got angry!

I looked up at the stars and said, "God, I am only 13 years old, how am I going to change this? God, are you there?"

I got really mad and began to pedal faster. I got home as quickly as I could. I skipped dinner and walked right up to my room. After a few minutes my mom came up the steps and pushed open my door.

She said, "James, what is wrong, sweetie?"

I said, "Not much."

I sucked in my tears. I pulled the pillow over my face to hide my tears of anger.

She sat on the edge of my bed and said, "Life can be challenging sometimes. It's not always a smooth path. You have to climb hills sometimes to achieve your goals."

I said, "Mom, I love you, but this problem... it

is unfixable."

Mom said, "There is one thing I learned in life so far."

I said, "And what is that?" all sarcastically.

Mom said, "Attitude is everything! You can be conquered by life, or you could conquer the world if you chose. It's all in your attitude. Think about it, James!"

I said, "I will, Mom."

Mom said, "Sweet dreams, sweetie," and shut the door.

I did think about what she said… I just did not know how to go about writing this book, this message God wanted me to write. No one is going to buy it anyway, I thought. I turned over and went to sleep.

It was Saturday morning and the weather was warm for November. The sun was out and the wind was blowing. I decided to pull out the ramps and do a little jumping to take my mind off of things for a while. I put the ramps about twelve feet apart. I got up some speed and soared through the air, forgetting all of my troubles. *Swoosh!* I flew the twelve feet with ease and landed on the landing ramp. I rode down the sidewalk and turned around. I decided to try something different this time. I was going to jump the ramps backwards.

What I mean by backwards is instead of going back to where I started from, I was going to use the landing ramp as the ramp and the ramp as the landing ramp. I began to pedal and got up some speed. I hit the ramp and began to soar into the air. A large gust of wind came and blew the landing ramp out of my way. I hit the hard concrete, causing my bike's front tire to pop and jam. I flew forward and flipped over the handlebars, heading down to the concrete. As I flipped in the air I landed on my feet, going into a mild run and finally coming to a halt. My Uncle Dean could not believe his own eyes. He was watching me through the window and had come running out to see if I was okay.

Uncle Dean yelled, "James, that was amazing... how did you possibly do that?"

I said, "Do what?"

Uncle Dean said, "I just had seen you land on your feet after flipping over the handlebars of your bike! That was incredible!"

I said, "Uncle Dean, it was dumb luck is all!"

Uncle Dean said, "Luck my ass; kid, that was a miracle. God himself was looking out for you! I mean you were way up in the air!"

I looked up at him and smiled and said, "Maybe."

Uncle Dean picked up my bike and said, "Don't worry about the bike; I will have it fixed tomorrow."

Uncle Dean rubbed the top of my head and said, "Come on, let's get inside."

He carried my bike to the garage and put the ramps away for me. I went inside and got myself cleaned up for the night. When I came out of the bathroom, I could hear my Uncle Dean talking to my mom.

Uncle Dean said, "James is a special boy. His jumping is incredible. He makes me look like a sissy when he's on that bike. He was so high into the air and when he landed, the damn tire just bent and blew apart. You should have seen him flip over the handlebars and land on his feet! I have never seen a front tire blow apart like that... It was like he had angels looking out for him."

My mom said, "Ever since he was young he has been in so many incidents. I don't think that's normal?"

Uncle Dean said, "He loves thrills and excitement is all. Hell, I did too when I was younger. Remember the river jumps?"

Mom said, "Yes I do, Dean; do not encourage James anymore!"

Dean said, "Oh Shannon, he will be fine; do not worry. I am looking after him the best I can."

Mom said, "I know you are. James loves the bike and ramps you built for him. I can't help but worry about him."

Dean said, "That's understandable, he is your son."

Mom said, "Do all you can to look after him... promise me, dammit!"

Uncle Dean said, "I am! He will be just fine. Hell, Shannon, he's tougher than I am. You heard what he did to two boys at one time. He should be looking after me."

Mom said, "He is...don't you see it?"

Chapter Five

# The Barn

I'd just turned fourteen and it was time for me to get a job. My friends were going to work at a local farm for the summer and I was going to be pretty much alone. Leslie was going to Europe for the summer and William went to his father's in California. He was going surfing! My friend Kyle hooked me up with a job at the last minute working with him and his family. Our job for the summer was baling hay and feeding the cows. After saying good-bye to my family, we headed out to the farm for six straight weeks. When we got out there Kyle showed me around the large barn. The barn had a conveyer belt that sent the bales of hay up to the loft area.

Kyle said, "From there it was stacked up to the ceiling in steps. By the end of the six weeks it will be full."

I said, "Wow!"

I looked up to the top of the rafters. It was high.

Kyle said, "Come on this way."

He opened the loft door and swung out on a rope. He slid down to the ground and said, "Come on; you're next!"

I jumped out onto the rope and slid down to the ground.

Kyle said, "That was pretty cool, huh?"

I said, "Yes, that was cool…it was a rush."

He took me to the bunkhouse to show me where we would be sleeping. It was a bunkhouse filled with eight bunks and it was attached to the side of the barn. It had an old phone, an old radio, and an old black-and-white TV. It only received two channels. That was it. Kyle's brothers and uncles were staying in there with us. Our first night was pretty funny, listening to those guys making fun of each other. They never said a word to me. They sure gave Kyle a hard time, though.

Kyle's uncle said, "You better get some rest, sweeties, because tomorrow is going to be a tough day."

Kyle said, "Okay, Uncle."

I said, "What does he mean?"

Kyle said, "Remember what I said about him. He likes to think he's a hardass."

I said, "He is doing a good job at it…maybe too good."

Kyle laughed a little and said, "It's okay, James, he's just playing with us."

I said, "I am going to take his advice and sleep. See you in the morning."

The next morning the lights went on! It was five A.M. and time to get ready to go to work.

Kyle's uncle said, "You two will be the throwers today."

Kyle said, "Oh shit!"

I said, "What?"

Kyle said, "It's the hardest job."

Kyle's uncle said, "It's best to start there so you can build up some strength."

I shrugged my shoulders and said, "Okay."

Kyle said, "We will be throwing bales of hay up to the back of the trailer."

I said, "How hard could it be?"

Kyle's uncle said, "I love this kid! We need more attitudes like his. Let's get going, fellas."

We walked out to the truck and climbed in.

Kyle said, "Try to pace yourself out here."

I said, "Okay."

The tractor began to cut and toss bales out to the trailer. We had to pick up the ones that hit the ground. Kyle and I began to pick up a bale together and set it on the back of the trailer.

Kyle's Uncle John yelled, "Faster, boys!"

We began to go as fast as we could. It was very difficult to keep up with the grownups. By seven A.M. I could not feel my back and arms. It was break time. Kyle was hurting pretty bad as well. He asked me how I was doing.

I said, "Sore as hell…pass the canteen, please."

As he handed me the canteen of water Kyle said, "I lost feeling in my back."

I said, "Me too."

I turned to look at the rising sun and saw someone walking towards us. It looked like an angel with the sun at her back with the sunrays protruding around her. I couldn't stop staring.

Kyle noticed her and said, "That's Chantelle."

Chantelle came to the field to bring us breakfast and more water. She worked at the farm full time with Kyle's grandma. Chantelle was beautiful. She had long brown silky smooth hair and an awesome figure. She had her shirt tied halfway up her waist and had on old worn-out blue jeans; her tan skin showed through the holes. I could not help saying "hubba, hubba" to Kyle. She made my heart race faster than any Corvette could go.

Kyle said, "She is off-limits to us all. Grandma's rules and she means business, I tell ya."

I said, "I did not meet your grandma yet."

Kyle said, "Do not worry; she will be there at dinnertime."

I said, "Cool."

I had a hard time not looking at Chantelle; she was stunning.

Kyle said, "My brothers have been drooling over her for two summers now. Wait until dinnertime, you will see my grandma in action."

Chantelle brought over my sandwich and a canteen of water.

She said, "Drink as much water as you can out here, James; you don't want to get dehydrated."

Her finger gently grazed my hand as she let go of the canteen. Her touch sent chills of excitement through my whole body. Chantelle then winked at me just before she turned away.

Chantelle said, "Don't work too hard out here, boys," and walked back to the truck.

I began eating my sandwich, watching Chantelle drive away when everyone began to laugh. I looked around to see what was so funny. Uncle John pointed at me and laughed some more. I had a boner and did not realize it. Kyle began laughing when he noticed.

Kyle said, "Don't worry; she has that effect on us all!"

He laughed some more with the rest of the guys. I was embarrassed a little bit, but not too much. She was attractive to me and after all, I was becoming a man. I shrugged my shoulders and continued eating my egg-and-sausage sandwich. Later that day Chantelle brought out our lunch. Grandma had made French onion soup bread bowls. They looked delicious. When Chantelle handed me mine she grazed my hand again with hers, then smiled. Her hands were so soft, it started all over again. I felt my jeans tighten up.

Chantelle whispered so softly, "Sit by me at dinner."

She turned and walked away. I quickly sat down and leaned over to enjoy my lunch without being laughed at. The French onion soup bread bowl was so delicious. After lunch we returned to work until the tractor broke down.

Uncle John said, "We are finished for the day, men!"

I was exhausted and my muscles hurt so badly. I had no arguments with stopping for the day.

Kyle said, "Come on, let's go swimming and cool off."

I said, "That sounds excellent!"

We returned to the bunkhouse and put on some shorts to swim in.

Kyle said, "Come on, I will show you where the pool is."

The main house was quite a ways away from the barn, at least a quarter mile away. By the time we walked there, I did not feel like swimming anymore. We both jumped into the water to cool off; it felt so refreshing. My body was so sore I could not swim. I sat on the steps with my entire body under the water. About an hour passed and the rest of the guys came to cool off.

Uncle John said, "Why didn't you two wait for us, you could have rode with us?"

I went to say "I don't know" but Kyle cut me off and said, "We were hot is all."

Uncle John said, "Kyle, you need to slow down and enjoy life, you are always in a hurry to be somewhere. Life is going to pass you by. When you're old you won't have many memories of it."

The rest of the guys said, "Hear! Hear!"

Kyle said, "Come on, Uncle. I am just having fun. Why are you always so serious all the time?"

The rest of the guys tipped their beer bottles together and said, "Cheers to Uncle John."

Kyle said, "I guess I love life so much I lit the candle at both ends."

I said, "Nothing wrong with that! Having fun is what life is all about."

Uncle John said, "I think having fun is great. Don't get me wrong, James. I just think you have to be serious when you're an adult."

Kyle said, "We are fourteen years old, Uncle; I am still a kid. Let me be one while I have a chance."

Uncle John said, "Back in my day I was doing this when I was twelve years old. Don't feed me that bullshit."

Kyle looked at me and said, "See what I have to put up with in my family, James. They don't want anyone having fun, it's all business all of the time."

I smiled at Kyle and said, "Be careful in what you

wish for. With all due respect to you and please don't take this the wrong way…be grateful you have a family that's looking out for you. Things could be a lot worse. You could have a life like mine."

Kyle sat there a minute and became a little angry.

Kyle said, "I realize these guys look out for me and I am grateful for it. All I am saying is lighten up, Uncle, I got the message, alright! Now let's have some fun."

We swam for a couple of hours and relaxed in the sun.

Kyle looked at me and said, "You're a good friend, James. Thank you for making me clearly see the differences between our families. I know you don't have much, which is why I asked you to come here. These guys can be tough to be around. Most of my friends are afraid to come around here. My uncle likes you, you know."

I said, "That's cool, I like them all too."

A little while later Uncle John stood up and said, "Everyone go shower off, it's dinnertime soon. We don't want to be late!"

Kyle stood up and walked out of the water.

He said, "Come on, James, I will show you where the shower house is."

We walked into a building right next to the pool just past the restrooms. It was a large shower room like you would see in a school locker room. They even had a towel laundry room. We got cleaned up for the night and walked back to the truck and waited for the rest of the guys. Kyle and I were so tired, we sat on the tailgate and lay back in the truck bed and fell asleep. We both woke up with our feet dangling from the tailgate. We were driving back to the bunkhouse to rest just before the dinner bell.

Kyle and I talked about girls for a while.

Kyle said, "Have you ever had sex?"

I said, "Kyle, I just grew pubic hairs like yesterday...so no I haven't had sex yet."

Everyone started to laugh at my comment, including Kyle. He seemed to have a good sense of humor.

Uncle John said, "You are a funny guy."

I said, "Thank you."

Uncle John said, "Kyle did tell you Chantelle is off-limits, right, just in case that boner comes back?"

Everyone started laughing at me again. I mean they laughed hard! I laughed with them.

After a few minutes Uncle John finally quit laughing and said, "You are a good sport, James...but seriously though...stay away from Chantelle. Grandma will kill you!"

Everyone started laughing again. I laughed with them. There was no way they were going to intimidate me. After all, I had never been with a girl before. My first and only thoughts about having sex were about

Chantelle, but I did not share that with the rest of the guys. There was something special about Chantelle and me. I felt a connection, and I must say it was powerful. Besides, she wanted to sit next to me at dinner. I had kept that to myself as well. An hour later the phone in the barn began to ring. *Ring! Ring!*

Uncle John said, "Mount up, boys, it's dinnertime!"

We all headed back to the main house in the truck. When we got to the main house Kyle introduced me to his grandmother and grandfather. Grandpa was super nice and Grandma looked like the sweetest old woman you would ever see until she spoke. Chantelle came in the room from the kitchen and Grandmother properly introduced us.

Grandmother looked me straight in the eyes and said, "James, Chantelle is off-limits, son. Okay, sweetie!"

She continued to stare at me eye to eye until I said, "Yes, ma'am."

Chantelle walked away and Grandma put her arm around me and said, "Come on, let me show you around."

The house was huge. They had a giant living room with four couches and Grandpa's recliner. It had a very large fireplace that you could see through into the dining room. Instead of a bearskin rug in front of the fireplace, they had a spotted black-and-white hide from a cow. It was really cool looking.

It was mostly country decor with a lot of cedar ceilings and trim.

When we approached the steps to go upstairs, Grandma politely said, "Off-limits to James. Come on, sweetie."

And we kept walking. After the tour of the kitchen, bathrooms, and the large family room, we were back into the dining room. We all began to sit down for dinner.

As I went to sit down in one of the chairs, Uncle John said, "James, we have assigned seating and this is your chair for the summer."

I said, "Okay, John."

I went and sat down in the chair. Chantelle came and sat down next to me. After Grandfather said grace, the table became loud with everyone's chatter. Chantelle carefully slid a note in between my legs, grazing my inner thigh. My first thought as my pants tightened up again was, "Oh shit, not a boner at the dinner table."

I turned to look at her for a very brief moment so no one would notice. Wow, was she beautiful. I could smell her hair… It smelled like fresh spring morning air. I think I was falling in love with her that very moment. She acted as if nothing had happened and began filling her plate with spaghetti. I began to calm down and felt my pants go back to normal.

After the great dinner, Grandpa said, "Boys, you had a good first day. Johnny, I am proud of you."

Uncle John said, "Thank you, Dad."

Grandpa started to talk smack about Kyle's dad because he was not there to help the family. I looked over at Kyle and he looked defeated by his facial expression.

Uncle John said, "That's not fair, Dad, he is not here to defend himself."

Grandpa said, "You are right! I apologize to everyone here at the table. Boys, family is all you have in this world! Respect each and every one of them! Go on back to the bunkhouse; I will see you in the morning! Johnny, the tractor is repaired."

Uncle John said, "That's excellent, Dad. I can't believe they fixed it already."

Grandpa said, "Don't be hard on the old girl tomorrow until the new one gets delivered. Run her at three-quarter power for a couple of days."

Uncle John said, "Alright, Dad, whatever you want."

Grandpa said, "When the new one comes we will make up for the time lost. Don't worry about it."

I carefully picked up my folded message and put it in my front pocket.

I said good night to Grandma, Grandpa, and Chantelle. Chantelle stared at me for a moment; we connected eye to eye. Right then my heart began to feel different. I smiled at her and turned to walk away. We headed back to the bunkhouse. I climbed inside my bunk and turned towards the wall. After everyone settled down, I carefully pulled out the note from my pocket and slowly opened it up. The note read...

James,

For some reason I like you a lot. I want to spend time with you this evening. I will come to the barn at midnight. Meet me in the loft. Don't let anyone see this note. You know what will happen.

Chantelle

I slowly folded the note up. I didn't know what to do with it. I sat there for a while thinking about where I could hide it, and then it came to me. I slowly started to rip up the note and eat it. It wasn't so bad. At least I did not have to worry about anyone finding it. We sat and listened to a ball game on the radio for a while. Uncle John finally shut down the radio and turned out the lights. I was so excited to be with Chantelle I could not sleep. About an hour later I slowly got up and walked to the door. I carefully grabbed the door handle and slowly opened it; it made the faintest squeaking noises. I turned around to see if I woke up anybody. Nobody stirred or made a sound.

I walked over to the barn entrance and walked

inside. It was so dark I could barely see my hands. I knew where the ladder was and made my way towards it. When I reached the ladder, I began to climb up into the loft. When I got to the top of the ladder I carefully stepped into the loft. I could hear Chantelle giggle a little and the loft door slowly swung open, revealing Chantelle in the moonlight.

She whispered, "James, I was not sure if you were going to show up. Did you like my letter?"

I whispered, "I did, and I feel the same way about you."

Chantelle whispered, "I knew we had a special connection."

I began to walk towards her. Chantelle began to walk towards me until we met face-to-face. Our lips touched ever so softly. It was the most romantic kiss. It was the perfect kiss. Chantelle slowly pulled away and reached down for my hand.

She whispered, "Come this way."

I did as she said and walked with her. We began to climb higher up into the loft on the bales of hay, level after level until we couldn't climb any higher. When we got to the top, we both sat down for a brief moment and then lay down next to each other. Without a word said, we began to kiss and touch one another.

Chantelle whispered, "Have you ever been with a girl before?"

I whispered, "No."

She whispered, "Well then, you will never forget me."

She smiled at me. I thought I would never forget her anyway even if I didn't have sex with her. She put her hand on my chest and then reached down to my pants and began to undo my belt. I was touching her breast and began to undo her shirt buttons. I untied the lower part of her shirt and slowly removed it. We kept kissing and removing each other's clothing until we were both naked. Well almost! I had a hell of a time trying to remove her bra. Damn those things, I thought. I gave up and pulled it off of her like pulling off a T-shirt.

Chantelle giggled and softly said, "You will have to practice."

She rolled me over onto my back. I could feel the hay poking me on my butt and my back. I didn't care, I was so focused on Chantelle. She reached down and gently grabbed me.

Chantelle said, "You are really new at this, aren't you?"

I said, "Yes."

She reached down and grabbed my hand and placed it on her vagina. She began to moan as I touched her. I caressed her more and more and finally went inside of her. The more I moved, the more she moaned...it got louder and louder. I did not say anything. Chantelle positioned herself above me and slowly sat down on me, until we connected. I couldn't believe my penis was inside of her vagina, and it felt awesome! This was really happening to me, I thought to myself. Chantelle began to rock back and forth on me while I touched her stomach and her chest. She shut her eyes and began to moan almost like a whisper. Almost like a soft love song. We both began to sweat like crazy. My heart began to race like never before. My face felt flushed! It felt so wonderful to have sex for the first time. I began to feel funny but in a good way.

I said, "I think I'm going to?"

When I said that, Chantelle came down to my chest and hugged me tight. She rolled us over to her back, not breaking our connection, and reached down and grabbed my butt and pulled on it hard and whispered, "Okay, James, let it go."

I looked at her in the eyes and then released inside of her. It was the most incredible feeling I have ever shared with another. When I was finished I lay on top of her breathing so heavily. We were both so sweaty and slippery. Chantelle finally let go of my butt and ran her fingernails up my back, causing me to twitch a little.

Chantelle said, "That was incredible, James."

I kept breathing heavily as I stared into her eyes.

Chantelle smiled at me and we kissed some more. I turned and lay on my side to catch up with my breath. Chantelle turned on her side and faced me to where our noses touched.

She rubbed her nose onto mine and said, "That is called an Eskimo kiss."

I said, "I like it when our lips meet."

I smiled at her and she smiled back. We kissed for a while and made love again and again.

A couple of hours later Chantelle said, "You have to be exhausted?"

I said, "I am very tired and sore now."

I turned to lie on my back. Chantelle slid over and put her head on my chest. I began to caress her and run my fingers through her hair. Neither one of us said another word; we both went to sleep.

The next morning I could hear Uncle John yelling, "James, where are you!"

I woke up and whispered to Chantelle, "Don't say a word. Stay here until we have gone."

Chantelle whispered, "It will be alright, please don't worry. Everyone knows I come here first thing in the morning to work out."

I got dressed as fast as I could. I fell down a couple times and jumped down off of the bales and walked over to the door of the loft and yelled, "I am up here, John."

Uncle John yelled, "What are you doing up there so early?"

I yelled, "I woke up a little while ago and my muscles were sore. I thought if I threw a few bales around it would help me loosen up."

Uncle John yelled, "Come down from there, we need to get going."

I turned to look up at Chantelle and smiled. Chantelle blew me a kiss. I smiled again at her and jumped to the rope. I spun around and around, sliding down to the ground.

As I approached Uncle John he said, "You are one crazy kid. Nobody works out before a hard day's work."

I smiled and did not say anything back. No one else even had a clue that Chantelle and I were together. Later on that day, Chantelle brought out breakfast for us. She did very well acting as if nothing had ever happened. When she brought me my sandwich and water canteen, she touched my hand and smiled at me.

She briefly raised her eyebrows up and down and then whispered, "Save some energy for later."

I smiled and said, "Thank you for the sandwich."

I knew all of the guys were watching me to see if I produced another boner. I looked at them all and smiled.

By the fifth week Chantelle and I made love wherever we could in the middle of the night, including the pool and the shower room. It was very hard during the day to not reach out and touch her. Chantelle had a very difficult time with it too. Kyle had become very distant and had kept to himself over the last two weeks. I would ask him if anything was wrong. He would just shrug his shoulders.

It was the last few days of the summer and Uncle John had put Kyle and me up in the loft to stack the remaining bales. Along the top of the rafters was a zip line with hooks to grab the bales with. Uncle John explained to Kyle and me how dangerous they were and to be alert at all times.

He lifted his shirt and showed us a scar from when he was a little boy. He told us the story of how he was goofing around and how the hook had punctured his stomach. He had my full attention. As the bales came up the conveyor belt, I grabbed them and hooked on to them with the zip line and pushed the zip line over to Kyle. For hours we did this until we were both exhausted.

After a brief rest Kyle said, "Let's do a couple more and we will finish up."

I said, "Okay."

I hooked on to the next bale and pushed it over to Kyle. I sat down waiting for Kyle's signal that he was pushing the zip line back to me.

Kyle never said a word and flung the zip line back at me as hard as he could. The hooks were facing in my direction and coming at me! I did not see it coming. Just before the hooks hit me, Chantelle came out of nowhere and tackled me down to safety. She hit me like a linebacker would during a Sunday football game. The zip line hooks stuck into the bales behind us.

I stood up, angry, and yelled, "Kyle, are you crazy?"

Kyle just stood there looking at me with a strange look. His blue eyes turned black and his expression was not his own. I thought, not again! He's here!

Chantelle stared at him and yelled, "Kyle, are you okay?"

Kyle did not say a word; he just stared at us both. I looked at Chantelle and asked her if she was all right.

Chantelle said, "I am, are you okay?"

I said, "I am."

She walked over and hugged me. We both turned to look at Kyle and he was gone. I called for him and he never responded. It was as if he'd disappeared into thin air. I quickly looked out the loft doors and he was nowhere to be found.

I said, "Thank God you were there, Chantelle; that could have killed me!"

Chantelle said, "Yes, I know; I did not see you all day so I thought I would come and check on you."

I took a deep breath and said, "I'm so glad you did."

I gave her a big hug and kissed her.

Chantelle said, "I'm going to miss you when you go."

I said, "I'm going to miss you too, I hope we can be together again soon."

Chantelle said, "Do you think anyone suspects us?"

I said, "I don't think so. No one has mentioned a word."

I sat there thinking about Kyle and why he would do that.

I said, "Did you see his eyes?"

Chantelle said, "Yes, they were black. The veins in his head and neck were black as well."

I said, "I know, it's crazy."

I waited a second and then said, "You better go back to the house, I will go and find him, and talk with him."

Chantelle agreed.

I said, "Let me go first."

I walked over to the loft doors and grabbed the rope and slid down. I looked around the barn for a while and then walked into the bunkhouse. Kyle was sitting there in his bunk looking at a magazine.

I said, "Kyle, are you okay?"

He said, "Yes I am fine, are we going to work today? I have been sitting here waiting for you guys to return."

I said, "Kyle, we were at work for most of the day; it's almost dinnertime."

Kyle looked up at me. I noticed his eyes were

blue again.

Kyle said, "Don't mess with me."

I said, "Kyle, we were at work most of the day. Maybe the sun or the heat has gotten to you."

Kyle reached up and felt his head and said, "I do feel warm, maybe I will lie down for a while."

I said, "Better than that, let's go to the pool to cool off."

Kyle said, "That sounds good, let's go."

I watched him like a hawk watching its prey. We changed into our shorts and headed to the pool. When we got there Kyle jumped in and cooled off. I sat at the steps and slowly slid down into the water to cool off. The hair on my neck stood on end. Something told me to get out of the water. Call it intuition, I don't know, but I followed my heart and got out quickly. Just as my foot left the water, Kyle was reaching for me to pull me back in.

In a very deep and dark voice Kyle yelled, "Where do you think you're going!"

I turned around and Kyle's eyes were black again. The veins in his head were black all the way to his neck. I slowly backed up to the gate and stood there staring at him, not knowing if he was going to attack me or not. Kyle stood there looking at me and did not say another word. I stood there ready to fight! I figured if the devil could not breathe, I might have a chance. I was going to punch him in the Adam's apple first!

I yelled like a man, "I do not fear you, Lucifer!!!"

At that very moment Uncle John and the boys came driving up to go swimming. I turned to look at them for a brief moment. When I turned back to look at Kyle, he was swimming and acting as if nothing happened. I looked up at the house, and there was Chantelle looking out of the window. She smiled at me and turned and walked away.

Uncle John said, "There you guys are."

I said, "Hi John, I think the heat has gotten to Kyle."

Uncle John said, "Kyle, are you doing okay?"

Kyle said, "It's like James said, I think the heat has gotten to me."

Kyle kept swimming as if nothing happened.

Uncle John said, "We finished all of the bales and we are going home earlier than planned."

My heart began to race at the thought. I did not want to leave Chantelle.

I said, "When?"

Uncle John said, "Right after dinner."

Uncle John looked at me and smiled and whispered, "You might want to spend some time with her before you leave."

I smiled back because I thought he knew, that I knew, that he knew, about Chantelle and me.

I sat by the edge of the pool thinking this whole

summer nobody knew about Chantelle and me. I was surprised that no one had said anything about it. I guess either way the work got done or that's all that mattered. That evening just before dinner I was the last to go shower and get cleaned up. On my way out of the shower, a familiar hand pulled me into the laundry room and shut the door. Chantelle began to giggle. She gave me a wonderful going-away present, but I don't want to share it with you. I will let your imagination go wild....

## Chapter Six

# My First Car

On the way home Kyle acted as if nothing ever happened. I knew who really was after me and why, but I could not let that stop me. I couldn't wait to talk to God again. I had more questions for him. Uncle John dropped me off at home and handed me an envelope with my summer's earnings. I said "thank you" to them and told Kyle I would see him soon.

Uncle John shook my hand and he said, "Thank you again for helping my family."

I said, "It was my pleasure."

Uncle John leaned forward and said, "I really never knew about you and Chantelle."

He winked at me. I smiled at him and winked back. I can only hope that he would keep it a secret for Chantelle's sake.

I worked at other jobs close to home over the next two summers. I never did see Chantelle again so far. She had moved on to college after that year we were together. Not another word was ever spoken about her. The girls that replaced her at the farm were beautiful, but not the same, Kyle said. I miss Chantelle's smile and her touch. I lay in bed that night thinking about God and where he had been. Not that he needs to check in with me. It had been a couple of years since I'd heard from him. I thought that was strange. I had so many things to thank him for—especially Chantelle! Man she was beautiful.

It was the beginning of a beautiful summer. I was 17 years old and just received my driver's license. I was very excited to drive my own car. I did some trading with my brother Jason and swapped him my dirt bike for a 1970 Plymouth Roadrunner. The car was in good running condition but needed some work on the body. My mom would not let me keep it at our house until I could put a license plate on it and insurance. My sister Lori and her fiancé Keith let me keep it at their farm just outside of town. It was the first weekend after school had let out and my sister was having a party at her house.

My friends were invited to come and hang out. William and Leslie, Kyle and Cindy were coming out there with me to stay the night. The party they were having was a field party. There was a small barn there for people to sleep in if they wanted to. Kyle seemed to be acting okay for the last two years. He never made any more attempts to kill me anyway. I had been keeping an eye on him. When we arrived at my sister's place, my friends were checking out the Roadrunner. It was pretty cool with headers and side pipes. Kyle jumped into it and started it up. He revved it up a couple of times to hear the pipes roar.

He shut it off and said, "Wow, this is incredible, James. I am so jealous of you right now."

I said, "Why?"

Kyle said, "Because you have a car and I don't."

I said, "Kyle, material things are overrated."

Leslie giggled a little bit.

I said, "Come on, the beer keg is open for business."

We all walked over to the bonfire and grabbed ourselves a beer. I introduced my friends to Lori and Keith. They all seemed to get along pretty well.

Keith said, "James, you owe me a ride in that beast of yours."

I said, "Keith, you can drive it anytime you want."

Keith said, "I already drove it. I would like to see you drive it though."

I said, "Okay, later on tonight."

Keith held up his beer and said, "To the birthday boy!"

Everyone tipped their plastic cups to honor my birthday.

I said, "Thank you, everyone."

Leslie gave me a hug and said, "I think your car is pretty cool."

I said, "Thank you."

I hugged her back.

I said, "It's not a Mercedes Benz, but it will have to do for now."

We all laughed together and pulled up a log to sit on to watch the fire for a while. I don't know if I said it earlier, but Leslie's family is really wealthy. More of my sister's friends came with more people. Hours later Lori came up to me almost drunk and was talking about some guy named Pete.

I said, "Who is Pete?"

Lori said, "Oops! I was not supposed to say anything."

I stood there looking at her until she spilled the beans.

Lori said, "Mom has a new boyfriend and wants to move in with him."

I said, "You're kidding me. When?"

Lori said, "Right away."

I said, "Where does this Pete live?"

Lori said, "In Waterford Township, about four miles from where we used to live on Lochaven."

I said, "That's cool."

I thought, I have not heard a word from Rosemarie or Paul in a few years. It would be good to talk to them again.

I said, "I wonder why she did not tell me."

Lori said, "I am sure she did not want to upset you."

I smiled at Lori and said, "Let's talk about it tomorrow."

Lori said, "Okay."

She walked away to greet more friends.

Leslie went to say something, sad I was sure of it; I cut her off.

I said, "Let's enjoy the night!"

William and Kyle said, "Hell yes!"

Kyle pointed to some older girls coming in. They walked away to go meet them. Leslie, Cindy, and I sat back down by the fire. We drank a couple of beers and had a few laughs on my sister. She was wasted and falling everywhere.

Cindy whispered, "I have a nice going-away present for you."

I said, "Oh ya, what's that?"

She rubbed my thigh and smiled.

I said, "Not tonight, okay?"

Cindy got frustrated and stood up and walked away.

Leslie said, "Why does that bitch think she can have any man she wants?"

I said, "Because she can, look at her. What guy in his right mind would turn her down?"

Leslie said, "You did!"

I said, "See, I told you I was messed up!"

Leslie pushed me a little and we hugged like good

friends do.

I said, "Besides, I am your date tonight, I promised not to leave your side."

Leslie smiled. Leslie was not the prettiest girl in school, but she was the sexiest girl I have ever seen. There was not a thing about her that was not perfect. She was a physically fit, 120 lb. absolute knockout! She has long black silky smooth hair. Her eyebrows were almost irresistible. She has these beautiful sexy green eyes. Any man would be so lucky to have her, I thought.

I said, "Since I am moving soon, there is not a person in this world I would rather be with than you, Leslie. You are my best friend."

Leslie said, "Oh, thank you, James. You are my best friend too! I just love you to pieces."

Leslie grabbed my hand and we walked back to my car. We stood next to it and finished our beers and talked.

Leslie said, "I have always loved you since the day I met you. You kicked that kid's ass and his friend. That was fucking awesome! Fucking bullies—I hate them!"

I said, "Well some people deserve their ass kicked. They were two of them. That's for sure."

Leslie said, "Can I tell you a secret?"

I said, "Of course."

Leslie said, "You were my hero that day. That guy just gave me the creeps, if you know what I mean."

I said, "I am flattered really…but thank you."

Leslie said, "I want you to be my first."

I stared at her for a minute.

I said, "Are you serious?"

She whispered, "Damn serious!"

We set our glasses on the hood and climbed in. Leslie began to show me how much she cared about me. I kept telling her no, that it was okay. Leslie wanted to please me. I finally gave in. I slowly kissed her and I must say it was incredible. It was like the time with Chantelle. I thought I would never be with a girl again like that.

Leslie whispered, "Have you ever had sex?"

I went to say "once" but Leslie kissed me again.

I whispered, "I don't think this is a good idea."

Leslie said, "Shhhh…"

She grabbed my crotch and began to rub it.

The windows steamed up fast. I locked the doors and turned on the radio for us. Leslie pulled me into the backseat. We pulled each other's clothes off and stared at each other for a moment. I sat back on the seat as Leslie climbed on top of my lap.

Leslie said as I touched her, "This is my first time."

I began to slowly masturbate her. Leslie became wet fast, and she slowly slid down on me, with her cherry bursting. We did not stop. The rest of me slid up inside her as she began to moan out loud. She acted as if she had done this before. She began to rock back and forth on me, moaning out loud. I let her do what she wanted. It was her first time after all. She continued to grind on me for a while, just totally enjoying herself. She kept her eyes closed and seemed to be in her own world. All I could think about was how beautiful she was on the inside. I thought I loved her. A moment later she slowly began to go up and down, breathing heavily. We both began to sweat like crazy. I pulled her all the way down on me and held her tight.

I said, "We should stop before I…"

Leslie cut me off and said, "No way. Shhhh!"

I said, "You don't want to get pregnant, do you?"

She hugged me tight and said, "Please do not stop, James. Please!"

She took another deep breath and said, "I am begging you, please… I am right there."

She slowly continued to go up and down on me. After a few minutes, I pulled her back down on me and held on to her tight until I released into her. I held her tight until I was finished. Leslie pushed on the headliner of the car, forcing herself downwards onto me, screaming, "Yes, James, yes!"

I felt her tighten up on me as she released her orgasm. I rested on the seat. Leslie slowly came down to my chest and I hugged her tight and continued to hold her. I kissed her head as she turned towards me, then our lips met again. Leslie slid down to my chest and I held her tight, kissing her head. We held each other for a while until Keith came knocking for his ride in the car.

I said, "It will be a while."

Leslie giggled and said, "A long while."

Keith said all drunk, "Come and get me when you're ready. Crazy, horny teenagers!"

Leslie and I looked at each other and laughed at Keith. I sat up and reached over to turn the dome light on. There was blood everywhere.

Leslie said, "I am so *sorry*, James."

I said, "Don't be. It's not a problem, I promise. Sit tight. Our clothes are dry, right?"

Leslie said, "Yes."

I jumped into the driver's seat naked and started the car. I wiped the windshield and side window enough to see out of and I slowly backed up all the way to the road. I shifted the car into drive and pulled away.

Leslie said, "Where are you going?"

I said, "To a safe place to get cleaned up."

Leslie said, "Where's that?"

I said, "You will see, please trust me."

Leslie said, "I do trust you, James."

I drove two miles up the road to an old farmhouse that was abandoned. I turned into the field where the cows used to be. I got out naked and opened the gate.

I ran back to the car and drove out into the field where the overhead storm shelter was.

Leslie said, "Where are you going to?"

I said, "All of these old farms have hand-pump water wells by these feeding overheads. I am sure there is one out here where we can get clean water from. Plus it's ultra-private. I have some clean towels in the trunk we could use to clean up with."

Leslie said, "You think of everything."

I said, "Not all of the time."

I pulled up to the shelter and there it was. I got out, making sure it worked. I lifted the handle and began pumping it. Ice-cold water came splashing out.

I said, "Come on, Leslie, its safe here."

I walked over and opened the trunk. Leslie shut the lights off and we used the running lights to bathe in and get dressed. I cleaned up the backseat while Leslie was finishing up.

I said, "See, no big deal!"

I rinsed off the towels and rung them out. I tossed them in the trunk and we headed back. Leslie and I held each other all the way back.

Leslie said, "It was just how I thought it was going to be, I love you, James."

I looked at Leslie and smiled and said, "I love you too."

I said, "Leslie, how do you feel about moving to

Waterford Township?"

Leslie sat there looking at me and did not say a word.

I said, "Think about it. I want you to be with me. We have been through so much together. I think my mom would be okay with you living with us."

Leslie said, "I will think about it. You know I am off to school soon."

We got back to the party and had a good time with friends. I told Keith another day perhaps for the drive. I never did like to mix drinking and driving together anyways. Besides, I wanted to be with Leslie. I had to try and talk her into moving with me. As the night progressed Leslie turned me down.

She said, "James, I have my whole family here and besides, I am going to college for my master's—you know this. Please don't make me feel any worse than I already do."

I said, "It's okay; school is more important anyways. Besides, we have the rest of our lives."

Leslie smiled at me and hugged my arm. Lori finally came clean about moving. Mom had already moved some things over to Pete's place. It looked like I was moving to Waterford Township, Michigan.

The next day I had a talk with Mom. She seemed relieved I was not mad about the new guy. I was happy for her that she found someone to share her life with. Pete seemed nice and we all got along that week. Friday came and I loaded all of my clothes into the car. My Uncle Dean moved in with my other uncle. It was going to be Mike and me and Mom and Pete. So I thought...

When I arrived at Pete's place on Pontiac Lake Road, he had five children he forgot to mention. So did my mom. Not that it was a bad thing...just a big surprise. They introduced them all and we sat down to talk. Mike and I seemed to get along with everyone well. I found out that only four of Pete's children lived there with him. It was going to be tight, back to the bunkhouse. We got settled in and began our new life in Waterford. Waterford was a party person's paradise. You name it...they had it!

I found in a short time that there were more women there than men—four to one ratio at the least. There was a party somewhere seven days a week throughout the year, parties for any reason. I did not participate in much because I felt like a sinner if I did. The truth is, I went to a few of them with my new friends Matt and Tony to check things out. I needed to know more about Waterford.

My trusty Roadrunner and I were making new friends quickly. Street credit meant something to this town, and reputation was another. There were hangout spots everywhere. If you went to the local carwash and you were looking for a good drag race, you could find one within ten minutes!

Needed someone to buy booze…no problem, everyone helped everyone there. You were a part of something special…a true brotherhood, I thought!

Matt, Tony, and I had a blast. We met people from all over the state that came there to have fun and be loved…and loved they were! The police turned a blind eye to the drinking and racing as long as no one got hurt. Who couldn't respect that?

We met people that had boats of all types. We swam and drank and swam some more! I lost all of my focus on what I was supposed to be doing… writing a book for God. I did not forget what I learned, I just put it on hold for a while to have fun. I mean I was still young. Another year had passed and I had turned eighteen and I finally heard from God again.

God said, "James, how are you?"

I said, "I'm doing well. I am having fun in Waterford!"

God said, "That's good, James. I apologize for not getting back to you sooner; there are many problems in the world that need constant attention."

I said, "I understand, it's pretty depressing to watch the news these days."

God said, "So tell me the progress you have made in your education to deliver my message."

I said, "God, I have so much to talk to you about. First of all I have had a few murder attempts on my life."

God said, "I am aware of the attempts, James. I am glad that you are safe and are doing very well to stay alive. My angels are doing very well to keep you safe and unharmed."

I said, "A few years ago, when I worked on the farm…I just wanted to know was Chantelle an angel?"

God was quiet for a moment and said, "She is lovely, isn't she!"

I said, "God, that doesn't answer my question?"

God said, "James, angels come in many shapes and forms."

I was quiet for a moment and then I said, "Thank you for her. I miss her deeply… is there any way I could see her again?"

God began to laugh and said, "She is busy handling other things now."

I said, "So, will I ever see her again? Please answer the question."

God said, "Yes, James, you will see her soon enough."

That was good enough for me.

I said, "God, I have continued my education on the balance of life. I have learned a lot on that topic. After watching a lot of news and educating myself in government politics at the library, I have learned that the greed is worse than I thought. The men that run our country and the world all are power-hungry and continue to want more; they fight over Earth's natural resources. It seems they will never have enough. The leaders of the world are so few; isn't there another way to eliminate the few that are corrupt?"

God said, "James, you need to open your eyes wider. This is why I sent you to Waterford Township. The people here live in sin daily. I wanted to put you in temptation to see how you handle it. There are many small towns like Waterford that need to change. The level of sin and greed is unacceptable. Learn as much as you can while you stay in Waterford. By the way the library there is excellent. They have books that you cannot find on the Internet. Go there and get started."

I said, "Okay. I will not let you down. There is no drug better than life in my eyes!"

God said, "We will see."

God was quiet for a moment and then said, "James, have you ever heard of a storm called a hurricane, tornado, typhoon, earthquake, or tsunami?"

I said, "I have, I know very little about them, why?"

God said, "I use these forms of weather to control a lot of troubles and problems that go on in the world."

I said, "Florida gets hit with a lot of hurricanes. So do Mexico, Texas, and many other areas in the Gulf."

God said, "Many men and women that live in those areas are repeated sinners. This is why I send so many storms in those areas. Mardi Gras must settle down soon. I will flood that city someday and everything in it. These people have forgotten my commandments. When you write your book, James, please include my commandments for all mankind to see and read, maybe add a small explanation or note next to them to better help them understand."

I said, "God, I will. That sounds like a good idea."

God said, "Please continue your education. I need you to learn as much as you can about the weather we just discussed."

God said, "One last thing before I go. I need you to learn everything you can about the Great Flood. Man needs to be reminded of my wrath! You can't move forward unless you know where you came from."

I said, "Okay, God, I will."

I sat there a moment trying to get the courage up to ask and finally I said, "God, why did you choose me?"

God was quiet for a moment and said, "I chose you for two reasons. The first reason is I chose you at your birth. You are very tough and a fighter, James, and I knew I would need your strength to complete the journey. The second reason was because of what you said in church when you were a little boy. I chose you because there is not another person ever to say such words and mean it, James. I chose you because your heart has touched mine and reminded me why I created man in the first place. In a way... man should be in debt to you."

I felt honored that he had chosen me. I was silent for a minute, letting God's words sink in, and I finally said, "Thank you, God."

God said, "James, get some rest, you're going to need it. Take it easy with those women. Have fun but not too much fun. Balance it out. Learn as much as you can, James; knowledge is power."

I said, "I will…thank you again. Good night, God."

God said, "Good night."

I lay there confused for a while and then it all made sense to me. I began to think about what I said in church when I was a little boy. I thought of God's Ten Commandments. I thought about what I would add that was brief and to the point. What an honor this is to be able to add to the Commandments. This is what I came up with…

## GOD'S TEN COMMANDMENTS

### 1. Do not worship other gods.

You shall have no other gods before me.

*James's note: (What God is saying is simple here…do not worship another. That's it, do not do it!)*

### 2. Do not worship idols.

You shall not make for yourself any carved image, or any likeness of anything that is in heaven above, or that is in the earth beneath, or that is in the water under the earth; you shall not bow down to them nor serve them. For I, the Lord your God, am a jealous God, visiting the iniquity of the fathers on the children to the third and fourth generations of those who hate me, but showing mercy to thousands, to those who love Me and keep My commandments.

*James's note: (Again...What God is saying is do not worship another. That's it, do not do it! Follow his rules!)*

## 3. Do not misuse God's name.

You shall not take the name of the Lord your God in vain, for the Lord will not hold him guiltless who takes His name in vain.

*James's note: (This one is huge; do not abuse this! You will be sorry!)*

## 4. Remember the Sabbath day.

To keep it holy, Six days you shall labor and do all your work, but the seventh day is the Sabbath of the Lord your God. In it you shall do no work: you, or your son, or your daughter, or your manservant, or your maidservant, or your cattle, or your stranger who is within your gates. For in six days the Lord made the heavens and the earth, the sea, and all that is in them, and rested the seventh day. Therefore the Lord blessed the Sabbath day and hallowed it.

*James's note: (See, you only have so much energy. Save it for Monday. Remember to respect thy Lord. Go to church if you're bored and appreciate your gift given to you: LIFE!)*

## 5. Honor your father and mother.

Honor your father and your mother, that your days may be long in the land which the Lord your God gives you.

*James's note: (This one is tricky. You read what I went through. If you must know I do honor my father and mother. We are humans that make mistakes. My answer to this is: we all make choices in life. Some are bad and some are good. I say focus on everything good! My father is paying his debt. I can guarantee he is begging for forgiveness! God handled it. Do not worry... No one goes unnoticed!) : )*

## 6. Do not murder.

You shall not murder, take another human's life and whoever murders will be in danger of the judgment.

*James's note: (This means it is not even healthy to think about it. In No way, shape, or form is this acceptable to God. Judgment is the last thing you want! I suggest you walk away and beg for forgiveness!)*

## 7. Do not commit adultery.

He who commits adultery lacks sense; he who does it destroys himself. He will get wounds and dishonor, and his disgrace will not be wiped away. For jealousy makes a man furious, he will not spare when he takes revenge. He will accept no compensation; he will refuse though you multiply gifts.

*James's note: (Have you ever heard the expression "tempted by the fruit of another"? If you ever get in this situation, break eye contact and run for your life! Trust me when I say, "You don't have enough money!")*

## 8. Do not steal.

You shall not steal. You shall not lie; neither shall any man deceive his neighbor.

*James's note: Do not take something you cannot pay for! (WARNING: There is a reason why this is in red! Give it some thought!)*

## 9. Do not lie.

The truth makes us happy and lies make us so sad. Lies hurt other people and they hurt us. There are times when we lie to get out of trouble. There are times when a lie seems to help. That isn't true. A lie always hurts the respect we have of ourselves and it usually hurts another person. A lie brings shame on us. A lie makes us sad. When you tell other people's secrets, even if they're true, that hurts them. When we make them hurt, we hurt ourselves.

*James's note: (This might sting a little. If you lie, your integrity as a person has no value! As far as I am concerned you are useless as a human being! Fix it immediately if you want someone to take you seriously and give you respect!)*

## 10. Do not covet.

You shall not covet your neighbor's house, you shall not covet your neighbor's wife, or male or female slave, or ox, or donkey, or anything that belongs to your neighbor,

*James's note: (What God is saying here is, do not have sex with your neighbor's wife or husband or live-in, your best friend's girlfriend or boyfriend. No man on man or women on women! No animals! Wake up, people! (Seriously, animal's!) I can see why God's mad! It's easy to meet the opposite sex.*

*Pay close attention to what I am saying! You walk up and say, "Hi, my name is James." (Just for example use your own name.) Make eye contact first. Do not stare at her breasts! Look her in the eyes and be genuine*

*and say, "I like you and I am attracted to you. Do you want to hang out and get something to eat or go watch a movie?" It worked quite well for me, maybe too good. I do know this! When you are genuine the opposite can feel it. Give it a try! If you are a guy and you stare at her breasts, all you are saying is you are hungry and you are a momma's boy or a male chauvinist pig! Either way it's Unattractive and you will fail!*

Learn them so you know them by heart. You will live well and have a peaceful life. You will not ever achieve a greater reward in life by not following the 10 Commandments. I have applied these to my life and they changed my life forever.

Back to why God chose me, it all came back to me very clearly. I was five years old at the time and Jesus was the topic that day in church. The priest had taught us what had happened to him and how he was betrayed by his friends closest to him. As the preacher went on with his lecture, I became angry and furious with the story being told to me. I've never felt so passionate about something since. I sat there very upset and frustrated that his friends would turn their backs on him, lie and let him be beaten and then murdered. The action I took that day is why God chose me. I stood up on the pew so everyone could see me. I then interrupted the priest and yelled, "Excuse me!

What cowards would leave their friend in need, especially Jesus! God's son! I would never do such a thing! I would fight until my death to have a friend like that!"

The preacher looked at me and we made eye contact. In silence he bowed his head at me. The room was so quiet you could hear my stomach growling from hunger. Everyone stared as I stood tall on the pew. I didn't want anyone to forget this moment. The moment was so powerful I seriously doubt that they did. Finally I sat down next to my little brother and my sisters and said, "Family is everything, Mikey, so are good friends. Don't ever forget what I said."

Mike looked up at me and said, "I don't understand what they did to Jesus?"

I said, "You would not understand; when you get a little older I will explain it."

Mike said, "James, please tell me."

I said, "They betrayed him and killed him because they were afraid and intimidated by him. He was different than everyone else. Jesus could do things they couldn't like heal people in many ways. God did a wonderful thing sending Jesus to earth to help man. Let's hope he will send another someday."

Mike said, "Do you think he will be stronger than Superman and have bigger muscles?"

I said, "I don't know, Mike, maybe?"

Mike said, "Church sure is confusing, could we go

home and watch cartoons now?"

I looked down at Mike and said, "Sure, let's go home."

Back in Waterford I spent the next year making new friends, new girlfriends too. I began to date a girl that was Jewish. Her name was Julian. When her parents found out that I was not Jewish, things didn't go so well for Julian and me. Her father despised me and could not tolerate the relationship we had. It did not last long for Julian and me. I did learn a lot about the Jewish community and culture, though. Everyone should visit the Holocaust Center at least once in their life.

What I didn't understand is if we are all God's children, what was the problem? Julian's father had a very poor attitude towards people that were not Jewish. I did manage to see him in action a few times when people came to his home to work on it. He treated them just like he treated me. I did not let Julian's father intimidate me after all the things I'd been through.

My question is… does he think he's better than I, better than God? I have learned very much in a short time about the balance of life. God created all men to be equal and to learn to respect one another, communicate with one another, trust one another, and rely on one another. It's time men apply this to their daily lives.

Lucifer and his advocates were working hard to challenge me again and again. Being tempted with drugs, many women, and the nightlife was not too much for me to handle. After Julian and I split up I began to spend a lot of time researching the Great Flood. For forty days and nights God made it rain. He flooded the earth to eliminate the sinners of the world. He had Noah build an Ark to keep alive two animals of every species to start over with. I personally do not want this to happen again. I can't begin to tell you how bad. The thought of spending roughly a few months on a boat does not sound appealing to me. I cannot even swim that good. Let's get things balanced out for him!

While spending time at the library, I met a new girl named Samantha. After a few weeks of dating Samantha, we were helping my stepbrother move to his new home in Novi. We dropped off our last carload and were driving home on Haggerty Road heading north. We'd just passed 14 Mile Road and begun to turn on the large curve ahead when my Roadrunner was struck by another car almost head on at a high rate of speed. If I had not swerved to the right, he would have hit us head on. Samantha and I did not have our seatbelts on when the car broadsided us.

As his Ford hit the side of my car, the gas tank exploded! *Boom!* It tore the car practically into two pieces, causing my car to spin out of control and into a field, throwing dirt, dust, and car parts everywhere. When the car came to a halt, I quickly looked over at Samantha to check on her.

I said, "Are you okay?"

Samantha said, "Yes, I am fine, just a little shaken up."

I quickly realized how lucky we were to walk away without a scratch. The only thing that happened to us is we bumped our heads together. People responded quickly to the scene. The crowd began to grow as Samantha and I walked up to the road to check on the other driver of the car that hit us. The man was passed out in his front seat. The West Bloomfield police responded quickly and were on the scene. A policewoman walked out to my car asking people where the driver went. I could hear her calling out for the driver and then call for the fire department. She watched as the back half of my car burned. Smoke rose high into the air. Samantha and I began to walk back to my car to tell the police officer it was mine. The officer got on her radio as we approached her and asked for backup, that the driver and passenger were ejected from the car in the field. All of a sudden it was as if God showed up himself and blew on the fire…the flames blew out… they were extinguished right before our eyes.

It made a large woofing sound! I could hear the sound of several trumpets ring through my head. I looked around but could not see anyone.

The officer said, "Did you just see that? I never had seen a gas fire go out like that!"

I ignored her and said, "The car is mine!"

She stared at the back half of the car while she quickly canceled the backup. She then turned to us and looked at me strangely. The officer looked back at the car and then back towards Sam and me as if she had just witnessed a miracle. She put one hand to her eyes and began to rub them. She shook her head back and forth a few times.

She said, "You are kidding me. Are you hurt?"

I said, "No, we are fine!"

Sam said, "We bumped heads is all."

She touched my arm and stared at me as if I were God himself, I felt.

She said, "You two are very lucky! I have seen many car accidents in my career, but none as bad as this one. I thought you two were ejected from the car!"

I said, "We heard you calling for the owner of the car and we walked back here."

The officer said, "Where did you go?"

I said, "We went up to the road to check on the other car involved."

The police officer said, "I checked on him when I first arrived, he is drunk and has thrown up all over his car and himself."

Samantha said, "That's disgusting."

The police officer looked at my car and said, "That is amazing the car did not blow you both up!"

She pointed and said, "That is your gas tank way over there. That man tore your car in two pieces. It looks as if he was trying deliberately to hit you. I can't believe you two are not hurt!"

She pointed upwards and said, "Somebody upstairs is looking out for you two kids!"

I said with confidence, "You could say that!"

The police officer said, "Come on, let's get this report over with."

We walked up to the patrol car with the policewomen. As we were finishing up our statements, the drunk woke up. He walked over to the other side of the patrol car and began to yell at us.

He yelled, "You lucky little bastard, I can't believe you're alive!"

He was wobbling back and forth.

Samantha said, "That is not nice at all!"

The drunk said, "Fuck you—you little bitch! You're lucky to be here with him!"

He tried to climb over the car to get to us but other officers tackled him and handcuffed him. He opened his eyes and they turned black right before us all. His veins turned black as well. It freaked out the police officers. It startled the woman officer when the drunk began to growl in this deep, dark voice. She drew her weapon and aimed it at him. She never said a word and continued to focus on his every move. The other officers tried to get the drunk under control. They wrestled with him for a minute. He was a lot to handle even with handcuffs on. Quickly, more officers came over to assist. They hogtied him on the ground and escorted the drunk away.

He yelled as they carried him away, "I will succeed next time, James. Next time!"

The woman police officer looked at me and said, "Do you know that man? What and the hell was that about?"

I said, "No!"

She looked at Samantha and then at me again and said, "How did he know your first name?"

Samantha spoke right up and said, "He must have overheard us talking."

I shrugged my shoulders. I was not saying a word!

The police officer said, "He had to have overheard us talking, he had to have? That makes sense."

She looked stressed about it. She finished up the police report and we waited for the tow truck to come. Samantha and I held each other as we stood close to the policewoman.

When the tow truck driver arrived he said, "How many died in this one?"

The police officer said, "No fatalities here."

The driver said, "You are kidding me?"

I said, "No, we are all okay."

The tow-truck driver began to pick up all the pieces to my car off the road and loaded them on his truck.

I walked over to the driver with the title and said, "Keep it; it's yours."

The driver said, "Thank you. This will take care of your bill."

I said, "Okay...thank you for cleaning it up."

The woman police officer said, "Climb in you two, and I will give you a ride to the edge of town."

We took her up on it. Samantha was quiet all the way there. We listened to the officer repeat over and over how blessed we were to survive the crash.

She said, "You guys are lucky."

I said, "We do feel blessed."

She drove us into Union Lake and we had her drop us off at the local Big Boy Restaurant.

We got out and said "thank you" to her for the ride. Sam and I walked into the restaurant and used the restrooms to get cleaned up a little and called for a ride home. Afterwards we sat down in a booth and I apologized to Samantha for the accident.

Sam said, "That guy was a freak! Did you see his eyes? I can't deal with that. I don't know what is happening here...but it's a little weird for me. James, after my father picks me up, I do not want to see you again. I can't handle this much excitement anymore. My hair is going to start falling out or something!"

I smiled at her and said, "Understandable."

I ordered us a couple of drinks and we waited for her father.

Jason came to pick me up. I quickly waved to him through the glass.

He walked in and slid down into the booth and said, "Are you okay?"

I said, "I am fine, carless; but fine."

Jason said, "Was it bad?"

Sam said in a very low and sad voice, "We should have not survived according to the police. The car caught on fire and there were car parts everywhere."

Sam's dad showed up. She slid out of the booth and said, "Take care, James."

She touched my hand and smiled at me for a brief moment and then walked away.

Jason said, "That badly?"

I nodded yes to him.

He rubbed my shoulder and said, "Let's go home."

We climbed into his car and he gave me a ride home. When I got back to the house, everyone had heard the news about the accident and was asking if I was okay. I explained what had happened to them in detail, except I left out Lucifer and his advocates' part.

(I tried to explain to my mom once and it did not go over too well. She stared at me like I was crazy.) They were all amazed as well.

The next morning Jason went out and bought himself a new car and gave me his old Nova to drive. I couldn't believe it. It was awesome.

As Jason gave me the keys and the title he said, "It is not much…"

I finished his sentence and said, "But it will do!"

I gave him a hug for helping me.

He squeezed me tight and said, "My little brother, I love you!"

I said, "I love you!"

Jason said, "You need some luck, kiddo!!"

I said, "I know it; I finally got called back for an interview at the car dealership."

Jason said, "That's awesome, when?"

I said, "Tomorrow morning."

Jason said, "That's great! See, your luck is turning around."

"Yes, finally," I said.

Jason said, "Enjoy the car, and I will see you later. I got to get home to feed the family."

I waved good-bye to him and watched him drive away.

My mom came out from the garage and said, "Here, this is all I have."

She handed me some money to help me get back on my feet.

Mom said, "It's not a lot, James."

I said, "Thank you, Mom."

She hugged me tight and said, "I am glad you are alive."

I said, "Me too! I am going to the library if anyone calls or needs me."

Mom said, "Okay."

She walked back into the house. While I watched her walk back in, I felt so blessed. I climbed into the old Nova and started it up. I began to drive to the library. As I drove I thought about how much my family loves me and how lucky I felt right then. I was going to miss my first car, though. I had so many great memories in it. It made me appreciate the little things in life that much more. While I read more about different secret codes, my focus seemed to be fixated on staying alive to finish the book. I thought, maybe I should be reading survival books instead? I also began to realize a little more how important this book was to God and mankind. What a day it was. Surviving that crash...I mean that car accident was unbelievable. It was a close call for sure. It sure is easy to get sidetracked, though, isn't it?

## Chapter Seven
# The Dealership

The next morning I was on my way to the car dealership for the interview. My family wished me
good luck on my way out. When I arrived, there was a
panel of three men and one woman interviewing me.

The used-car manager said, "My name is Jerry
Bernard. This gentleman here is Mike Clifford. And
this gentleman here is Lawrence Mildo. The lovely lady
is Bambi Borest."

I said, "Hello, everyone"—all calm.

Jerry said, "This is your interview for the used-car
porter position. Do you have any questions before we
interrogate you?"

I looked at him funny and shook my head no.

Jerry said, "Very well then, let's get started."

They all looked at me with intense looks on their
faces. Mike and Larry put on dark sunglasses while
Jerry pulled on his leather gloves. I thought, what is
wrong with these guys? Bambi sat back in her chair;
she looked all serious and sassy.

Jerry said, "Okay, first question. Do you have any
bad habits?"

I sat there a second and finally said, "What kind of bad habits?"

Jerry said, "The kind that ends up in jail?"

I quickly said, "No negative."

Bambi said, "How about girl issues... like keeping a girlfriend?"

I thought... what in God's name does this have to do with washing cars?

Larry said, "Where did you get your cooking degree? Also, do you have a specialty dish?"

I stared at them all. I went from one person to the other. I didn't know what to say.

Mike said, "While you're doing our laundry...you are trained to do laundry, right?"

As I went to say "I don't think this job is for me," Jerry stared at me all serious and started to laugh. The rest of the guys began to laugh real hard.

Jerry removed his glasses and gloves and said, "Your Uncle Dean put me up to it, kid! Man you looked scared."

I began to breathe and laugh with the crew.

Jerry said, "Could you start right now?"

I said, "Yes."

He stood up and said, "Come with me, James, I will show you around."

Mike and Larry said, "Welcome aboard, kid!"

Bambi said, "Welcome, James, we are glad to have

you. Your uncle said you were a lot of fun to be around."

I said, "Thank you."

I continued to walk with Jerry. We got around the corner and went into Jerry's office. Jerry picked up the phone and called my Uncle Dean at work and told him I showed up. They laughed for a minute and then hung up the phone. Jerry began to show me around.

Jerry said, "We start at 8 A.M. every day, James. Do not be late. If you are going to be late, please call me so I do not plan something and you are not here to aid me. Time is everything in this business, James."

I said, "Yes, sir!"

Jerry said, "Please call me 'Jerry.' Calling me 'sir' does not fit. In fact every time I hear the word 'sir' I start looking for my Marine drill-sergeant father."

What could I say, that was how I was raised to say? Life sure was confusing sometimes. He shook my hand. There was something special about Jerry, I just did not know what it was yet. He showed me where my equipment was and my duties. My duties included washing cars in and out and keeping the lot clean and weed free at all times. Rotate the manager special car daily. (That was to make it look like it sold.) Retrieve and hand in any items found in the cars during trade-in and whatever else Jerry thought benefited him and the crew. I took my sweatshirt off and went to work.

My new job title was "lot manager." It sounded a

lot better than car porter. Jerry did not mess around either. Being a person of your word meant something to him and the crew. He gave me a base salary of eight hundred dollars a month to start plus bonuses. It was a fun job. I did it all, from washing cars to removing stereos. Giving people rides home and picking them up for service. The tips people gave were generous too. I shared them with the crew as they did with me. We became a family instantly. My first year there was really nice. You name it, I drove it. It was any kid's dream job—that loved cars anyway. My favorite car... The Corvette! Oh my God, are they a lot of fun!

It never bothered anyone when I would read my books on my breaks, even when I ran over the time, which was a lot. The car lot was a busy and happening place. People came from all over the state to buy cars from them.

As time progressed, Waterford was just like a lot of towns in the world—people having as much fun as they could and letting it get out of control. Nobody was doing anything about it. Not even the police seemed to care too much. I did all I could to focus on the books. But I had to survive too. Working hard at the dealership was the only way for that.

About a year later I started to date a woman named Nancy. I met Nancy when her father had purchased a car for her from the dealership. She needed help with understanding the controls and I was asked by her father to go out and help her. I went out to help her as any gentleman should. When I introduced myself, we stood there talking about each other the whole time. Her dad would look out the window to check on us every thirty seconds, it seemed like. Nancy would give him a look.

I could picture Jerry saying, "James is a good kid! Do not worry! He will take good care of her!"

I finally got around to explaining the car's features. As I showed her the car, we were becoming very attracted to one another. We exchanged phone numbers right in the front seat of her new car and that was that. Her car was in need of some air-conditioning repairs, so we sent it out to the repair shop. When she came with her dad to pick it up the next day, the guys told me she was way out of my league and wanted to bet me I could not get her number at least… (Little did they know we were already dating each other? We went to dinner the night we met. Was it my fault they assumed?)

Jerry said, "I got twenty bucks James says that you cannot get her number before she leaves."

I smiled and said, "You're on!"

Mike said, "I want on this action. Twenty bucks, kid! Let's see what you got. I want to see you kiss her before she leaves!"

I said, "Okay… I will take your money."

Jerry said, "Shit, James, if you kiss her I will give you a $100 bill!"

Bambi came up and said, "Me too, sweetie… she is way too hot for even you."

Mike yelled, "I'll throw in a hundy, James! She's way too much for you, kid! Even you have to realize that."

I didn't know what to do other than talk a little smack back. So I said, "Bambi, I am going to make you eat those words… Mike… just watch the kid in action! Pay close attention to my every move. I am going to dazzle you all. Maybe even you will get laid this decade with these moves….they're that effective!"

Everyone began to laugh at me. They all huddled together in the corner window like a bunch of school kids watching me go to work. Nancy got out of her dad's car and he drove away, waving good-bye to us. We waved back and I began explaining to Nancy about the bet. Nancy loved it. As I began to walk her to her car, she slipped her arm around mine and held on to it tight. We laughed all the way to the car and stopped. I handed her the keys and opened her door for her. She set her purse on the seat and turned around. We both looked back at the onlookers and smiled like we were being filmed in a movie.

I even winked at them, hoping to grind it in some more. We heard a thud against the glass from inside.

We hugged each other for a few minutes to torture them slowly as they watched. We whispered about where we were going for dinner that night. Then it happened… Nancy and I kissed like you were watching your favorite movie on the big screen. It was so soft and passionate, it even made Bambi cry. We could faintly hear the guys clapping inside. We let go of one another and kissed one last time like we were never going to be together again. Slowly we let go of one another. I tugged on Nancy's lip with my teeth and gently let it snap back. Nancy climbed into her car and drove to work. I walked in the back door and the team was clapping like I had just won my very first award for best actor.

As they clapped Jerry said, "I will never doubt you again."

He handed me $120.00.

I said, "Thanks, boss!"

Mike was still clapping and said, "You are a true artist, kid! Wow! Way to go! I got schooled today!"

I said, "Thank you, Mike."

Mike also handed me $120.00

Bambi was still crying and gave me a hug.

She whispered, "You were right… there is no one too good for you. That was so beautiful and I loved every second of it. You should be in Hollywood, James. That was so hot…."

She too handed me $120.00.

Jerry said, "Now that you're rich, it's your turn to buy lunch."

I said, "No problem, I will take care of it."

Bambi whispered, "I will pay for it out of petty cash. Just get me the receipt, sweetie."

Jerry yelled from his office in the back, "I heard that, Bambi!"

I said, "Okay."

Bambi whispered, "Just go… don't worry about that sore loser."

I said, "Okay."

I made my way to the restaurant. Anyways… She was pretty easygoing at first. The guys and Bambi had their fun with her too, making her jealous all of the time. She would stop in on her break from the bank looking for me, and they would say he is helping this woman or that woman.

"How does he have time for you?"

Bambi would pretend I was under her desk all the time rubbing her feet and well… other things. Bambi intimidated Nancy. Bambi was a beautiful blonde-haired woman with a nice figure for an older woman. I am sure she could have any man she wanted. Later that year I was inside during a rainstorm and figured out why they had a woman like Bambi around. This older couple came in to buy a Caprice wagon. The old man decided no, they did not want it, but his wife did. No matter what Jerry said he could not close the deal.

Jerry said, "Wait one minute please so I can check with the boss."

The old man said, "Whatever, Jerry!"

Jerry walked back into Bambi's office for a moment.

Bambi came out and winked at me and said, "Watch and learn, kid!"

Jerry said, "Pull up a chair, James."

So I did. I sat there quietly and watched Bambi walk around the corner. The old man went nuts over her. He stood up to introduce himself to Bambi and wiped his mouth with his sleeve. He was literally drooling over her.

Bambi said, "So, you do not want that handsome wagon?"

The old man sat there shaking his head back and forth no.

Bambi said, "You would look very handsome be-hind the wheel?"

Bambi hiked up her skirt in front of the old man just a little bit. He crossed his legs immediately.

Bambi said, "I love a man that drives a wagon. There is something sexy about it me and my friends love."

He said, "Sold, I will take it."

He signed the RD-108 form (purchase agreement) for the asking price and wrote out a check.

I smiled at her and Jerry because it was exciting to watch the pros at work. Those guys were good.

Afterwards Jerry said, "What did you think, James?"

I said, "Selling cars looks like fun."

Jerry said, "Keep watching and learning. When you get about twenty-five we will put you on the floor."

I said, "Okay."

I was not sure it was for me, but I thought I would try when my turn was up. A year and a half later, Jerry came up to me with a proposal. He was leaving the company for good and wanted me to come with him. He explained what my new job would be in great detail. It was called an auto wholesaler's position. We would buy a car from one dealer and take it to another to sell it or sell some in the local paper or Internet. It sounded simple enough. He told me how much money was there if we worked hard. The thought of being on the road so much bothered me because of the accident situation. So far, I had had good luck avoiding Lucifer and his cronies. I could not let that control my life, though, so I agreed to quit and go to work with him. After a year of moving budget cars $10,000.00 and under, we moved up to mostly highline cars. I was blessed with this job, I thought. We worked hard and we earned it. I'd always wanted to drive a Ferrari. One day Jerry surprised me with an older Dino that he had bought. It was so cool. I didn't want to get out. At the time it felt like the fastest go-cart in the world.

We drove that car everywhere. Jerry finally was concerned as the mileage quickly added up. He decided that it was time for it to go. After the Dino was gone, we began to move a lot of Porsches. One day we were driving down Telegraph Road in Southfield approaching I-696 where it goes into four-lanes wide when we stopped at the light at 12 mile Road. I was the fourth car back from the light and on the far left side. I was driving a bright red 944 Porsche coupe. As I sat there waiting for the long light to turn was when a feeling I had not felt in well over a year returned. The hair on my neck stood up on end. I could feel the danger coming, and coming fast!

I slowly looked around; I had nowhere to go. Cars were everywhere! I started to panic as the feeling inside of me turned explosive! Jerry was sitting there next to me reassigning titles. He had his reading glasses on and looked relaxed.

I yelled, "Jerry, do you trust me?"

He said, "Explicitly!"

I said, "I hope that means yes!"

Calmly Jerry said, "It does."

I said, "By the way, where did you learn all of those big words?"

Jerry said, "I went to college for five years to be an English teacher. I have a bachelor's degree and my teacher's certificate and I am currently working on getting my master's."

I said, "How and the hell did you end up a used-car manager?"

Jerry said, "It paid better. And I do not have to put up with those babies."

I said, "Nice."

There was a large group of cars coming from behind and we were the fourth and last in line. I could not go anywhere. No one was behind us except for the cars approaching me fast.

Jerry said, "What's going on?"

I said, "Put your seat belt on. It's the law anyways."

Jerry said, "You're right."

I heard his seat belt click. I watched as the cars from behind got closer and closer. The hair on my neck was standing tall!

Jerry said, "James, are you okay?"

I did not take my eyes off the approaching cars and I nodded yes to Jerry. I put the Porsche into first gear. A large Buick was coming at a high rate of speed. As it got closer I dumped the clutch and jumped the Porsche up and over the curb, blowing out the driver's side tire. *SMASH!!!* The large Buick smashed into the Thunderbird that was in front of us, smashing it into the car in front of it. The rear end of the Buick rose into the air and then slammed down to the ground. All you could hear were tires screeching to a halt!

Jerry said, "Holy shit!!!"

Glass was flying everywhere! As the cars came to a stop we got out to help the injured. For some reason Jerry changed his mind and began to change the tire instead. I continued to walk towards the wrecked cars to help if I could.

Jerry yelled, "Do not get involved!"

I ignored him.

Jerry yelled, "James, wait for the police and ambulance. Do not touch anybody!"

I said, "Okay."

I noticed the woman driving the large Buick had dark black eyes and was trying to open her door. She punched it first and then tried to kick it open. She seemed so desperate! My first thought was... not again!

In the same dark deep voice I had heard before she kept yelling, "I will get you! I will get you!"

But the door was jammed, thank God! I mean literally! Her head was bloody and she had dark veins on her face as well. I decided not to listen to Jerry. My heart told me to help these people. I helped the other two people that were involved get out. Their doors were jammed and they were trying to climb out their windows. I helped them to their feet. The police had come quickly. I was so relieved the crazy lady was still stuck in her car.

I looked back at that freak and said, "Jerry, we got to go!"

Jerry said, "What, why?"

I said, "We need to leave right now! You don't understand. Please trust me!"

Jerry said, "Hold on, James!"

He put the flat tire and tools in the hatch and walked over to one of the police officer's. He asked if it was okay for us to leave and explained how we had a flat tire is all.

The officer said, "Of course, you were not involved."

Jerry came back and said, "We are okay to leave. Did you see that lady? I mean what a freak show!"

I said, "What lady?"

I was trying to ignore him.

Jerry said, "The lady driving the Buick!"

I said, "Yes, why?"

Jerry said, "She looked like a damn freak with black eyes, dark veins with blood all over. She was screaming something at me as I walked past."

We climbed into the car. I started the Porsche and slowly drove off the grass into the northbound traffic.

I said, "Jerry, I am sorry about the tire and rim."

Jerry said, "I am not. You saved my life! Thank you for that!"

I said, "You're welcome."

Jerry said, "I am curious though. How did you know the car was going to smash into us? That lady would have killed us both."

I said, "I don't know, my hair on my neck stood up and I felt like we were in danger!"

Jerry started making fun of the old *Lost in Space* by saying, "Danger, James Martin, danger!"

He began to mimic the robot. We both laughed a little. Not too much, though, because I loved that show.

In fact, I said, "I loved that show too, Jerry."

He stopped immediately.

He said, "That was incredible what had happened back there."

I said, "I know."

Jerry said, "How did you know?"

I said, "I do not know, call it really cool driver's intuition?"

Jerry said, "Okay, which sounds good for now."

We picked up Jerry's Corvette and dropped the Porsche off at the tire store to be repaired and drove home.

That night Jerry called me at 10:00 P.M. and said, "James, now I remember what that old lady was screaming at me as I walked by her."

My heart fell through the floor as I said, "Jerry, let it go please."

Jerry said, "I couldn't because she knew your name. She kept saying 'I am going to kill you, James Martin' over and over."

I said, "Please, Jerry, let it go."

Jerry said, "You owe me that much, James, how did she know your name?"

I said, "Do you believe in God?"

Jerry said, "Of course!"

I said, "Do you believe in the devil?"

Jerry said, "Yes, you have to. You can't believe in one and not the other."

I said, "Okay, cool…I couldn't talk here, it's not safe. I will speak to you in the morning. I will be there early around 7:00 A.M."

Jerry said, "Okay, I will see you then."

The following morning I sat down in Jerry's Corvette and said, "Good morning."

He said, "I did not sleep too well."

I said, "Let's go get some coffee; you are going to need it. You might want to stop and get a pint of something as well."

Jerry said, "I can take it, I am a big boy now."

I said, "I will remember you said that."

We drove down to the doughnut place and went inside. I started to explain to Jerry about my situation and then remembered that God said do not tell anyone. So I decided to leave out a few parts of the tale and explained to Jerry that since I was a little boy the devil has been after me for whatever reason I did not know. I left out the part about being God's messenger. I was not lying in my eyes. I continued to explain that he had made many attempts to kill me since I was five years old.

Jerry said, "I wonder what for?"

I had to lie to protect God. So I did and said, "I don't know. Maybe I am possessed is all? Would you have hired me if I said the devil is after me?"

Jerry sat there eating his doughnut and stared at me. I sat there feeling horrible that I'd lied and then all of a sudden I felt relieved. I could not explain it other than God was sitting next to me and made me feel better. I figured Jerry would understand once the book was finished. Either way, he was going to have to wait. I started to feel uncomfortable that he was not saying a word.

I said, "Jerry, I understand if you want to let me go. I mean most people would be scared. I'm sure there will be other attempts."

Jerry said, "Not a chance, I'm not afraid of the devil either!"

I said, "Thank you, Jerry."

Jerry said, "For what, as I am sorting through my feelings here I feel honored for some reason just to be a part of your life."

I reached up and shook his hand. I felt so grateful to have a friend to look out for me for a change. At times I felt very alone and singled out my entire life. And just like that Jerry let it go.

Jerry said, "Come on, let's get to the office and get out on the road. Today, James, it is a special day."

I said, "Yes, why is that?"

Jerry said, "Because today we are hooking up with the FBI in Detroit to purchase their seized used vehicles."

I looked up at Jerry and said, "Are you crazy! Why would you want to buy a drug dealer's vehicle?"

Jerry said, "I don't know why, but it sure is exciting, isn't it!"

I sat down in Jerry's Corvette. I sat there thinking how exciting this job has been and how it continues to be. I think Jerry lost a screw yesterday when I hit the curb. Buying seized drug dealers' cars is crazy, I thought. My first thought was when they got out of jail. Wouldn't you want your $50,000 car back? What if they hid something in it?

Jerry climbed in the car and handed me his briefcase. He told me to open up the briefcase and look at the folder on top. I opened it up and saw a picture of what looked like a brand-new white Corvette convertible.

Jerry said, "What do you think?"

I said, "Are you buying this?"

Jerry said, "I already did, that's our new office!"

I continued to look at the pictures while Jerry drove us to Detroit. When we got there, the car was beautiful. It was a white Corvette convertible and had black leather interior. It also had white BBS wheels on it and it seemed to set the car off perfectly. We waited a while and finally met up with the director of the FBI and finished up the deal. Jerry agreed to purchase all of the vehicles as they came in.

Jerry tossed me the keys to the new Corvette and said, "I'll meet you at the office in Plymouth."

I said, "The previous owner is in jail, right?"

Everyone began to laugh at me.

The FBI director said, "Don't worry, son, he is in jail for life."

I said, "That may be true, sir…but I know enough that he has friends."

Everyone stopped laughing.

The director said, "Just for some peace of mind, James, the car was thoroughly searched for drugs and cash."

I said, "Thank you, that does help, but I will be on the lookout."

Jerry said, "I think you have bigger worries to think about than these guys… especially after yesterday."

I said, "That is true, Jerry. See you in Plymouth."

The director said, "What happened yesterday?"

Jerry said, "James avoided an accident is all. He is a great driver."

I was not sure what Jerry had said to the FBI, but I was not waiting around to find out. I walked downstairs and grabbed my briefcase. I installed my dealer tag and headed back. The new portable office was pretty cool. It was very fast too. They must have modified it a little. When Jerry got back to the office in Plymouth, we transferred the rest of our equipment into the car and set it up for the next day. Our first day in the office was very nice. The Corvette had 900 miles on it and was like brand-new.

Jerry said, "So what do you think so far?"

I said, "Jerry, this job is any young man's dream, and I am living it!"

Jerry smiled and said, "You deserve it, James."

I said, "Thank you, boss!"

We had a great summer that year. Jerry had bought and sold a lot of highline cars. I even got to sit in a new Lamborghini with the engine running. I was tempted! It was not mine to drive, though. The car belonged to Jerry's friend Terry.

Terry said, "James, you can think about it; but don't do it."

I turned off the engine and slid out the keys.

I climbed out of the Diablo and said, "I was

tempted, Terry."

Terry said, "I could tell."

We continued to look at it.

Terry said, "James, write me a check for $225,000 and it's yours."

I handed Terry the keys and said, "Lamborghinis are overrated, buddy."

Terry looked at Jerry with disgust.

Jerry said, "What can I say? He's a Corvette man now."

Terry shook his head back and forth and climbed in his Bull car and took off. I must say that they do sound really cool...

The fall was here and I spent most of my time at work or at the library. I was doing my best to stay away from Nancy and really put a solid effort into the book I had to write. She was a huge distraction! Jerry was really flexible when times were slow and let me be. The more I was gone, the further Nancy and I faded apart and called it quits. I was at the Waterford library writing down some notes to use for a later date when I met a new woman by the name of Jillian.

Jillian said, "Hello, is this seat taken?"

I looked up at her and then quickly around the room. There were plenty of empty tables.

I said, "Why no it is not...please."

I stood up as she pulled the chair from the table.

She sat down and smiled at me. I sat back down and focused on my notes.

Jillian whispered, "I hate deadlines. Do you?"

I looked at her and said, "I... I guess so."

Jillian said, "Work can be so stressful at times."

I said, "What do you do for a living?"

Jillian said, "I sell networking and advertising ideas to companies."

I said, "That sounds interesting."

Jillian said, "What do you do?"

I said, "I sell cars on the wholesale market and some retail. But mostly wholesale. I work for a private dealer/collector in Plymouth."

Jillian said, "That sounds like fun."

I said, "It is very exciting at times."

When I said "it is very exciting at times," I was thinking about the time when Jerry was driving this old hooptie car and ran over some large orange road barrels one time when I was kind of hung over. He scared the shit out of me as they bounced off of the windshield, making a loud popping sound.

Jillian said, "My name is Jillian Foster."

I stuck out my hand and said, "My name is James... James Martin."

She touched my hand and I could feel her attraction in her heartbeats. She was excited to meet me as I was excited to meet her.

Jillian held on to my hand and whispered, "I am in town for a while with work, and do you want to have dinner with me tonight?"

I whispered, "That would be great. I know of the perfect place. Where shall I pick you up?"

Jillian said, "I rent a place in Clarkston Bluffs. Do you know where that is?"

I said, "I do."

Jillian said, "I live at xxxx Clarkston Bluffs Drive in the back."

I said, "I will see you at seven?"

Jillian said, "That is perfect."

She stood up and let go of my hand. I immediately felt naked without her touch. Never before had I felt this way."

Jillian softly said, "Bye, James."

I said, "Talk to you soon."

Jillian was a stunningly beautiful woman with straight blonde hair and the softest blue eyes that I have ever seen. She had a figure that would make any man stare and any woman jealous. Our first date together was perfect... maybe too perfect. If I liked something she liked it as well. It did not matter what the topic or category it was. If it was camping, she loved it too. I must say she had all of my attention.

That night I arrived a few minutes late. I was driving a used Corvette from the lot. It was an older 1973 big block coupe with side pipes and candy-apple red paint. I got out and went to the door. Just as I went to push the doorbell, Jillian had opened the door. The timing was a little strange.

She said, "I heard you pull up. That's a loud one."

I said, "On that particular car it's supposed to be. It's a car from the lot. I don't own a car myself, I drive the ones we have at the lot. It keeps the batteries charged and them running properly."

Jillian reached for my hand and we slowly walked out to the car staring at each other.

I opened the passenger door for her and said, "Watch out for those side pipes. They are very hot!"

Jillian said, "I can feel the heat from here. Is this car safe?"

I said, "Well…it's an older model but it should get us to dinner and back."

Jillian said, "I trust you, James."

She kissed my cheek and hiked her skirt up and slid down inside the car. Yes, I noticed she was not wearing any stockings…she was stunning!

I said, "Good."

She reached out and pulled the door shut. I walked around and got in. I felt the night was starting off great! I started the car. It was so loud you could not hear yourself think. I smiled at her and she smiled back. I slowly let out the clutch and away we went.

Jillian took an instant liking to the Corvette. She loved the power of it as it pushed her into her seat as I accelerated. Her legs captured my attention quickly while we drove. When we arrived at the restaurant, the valet parking attendant helped Jillian out of the car by placing a hot mat on the car's side pipes so she would be safe. There was a trick to getting out unharmed. Once inside we talked all night. It wasn't that normal chat like most dates. Jillian was different. We talked about life and family and even how many kids we wanted. We both said one. That night at her door, we kissed our first kiss. Our souls connected and all I could think about was being with her and never wanting to leave. There was something about her I wanted, and I must say there was something special about her I feared as well. After a few dates she captured my heart. We began to spend a lot of time together. It was time that was precious to God and to Jerry.

Jerry pulled me aside one day at work and asked, "James… are things going okay?"

I said, "Things are fine, why?"

Jerry said, "Well you have been coming in a little late, and leaving a little early. You don't want to hang out anymore and you don't want to work Saturdays anymore either."

I said, "Well, I have met a new woman and I have been spending time with her trying to build a new relationship. Working on my studies as well… you know I like to read."

Jerry said, "I could understand that. I thought maybe you got into drugs or something."

I said, "Not a chance! Let's do dinner Saturday night at the steakhouse by your place. You and Mrs. Jerry can meet Jillian."

Jerry said, "That sounds great."

That weekend we met Jerry and Donna at a steakhouse close to their home in Highland, Michigan. I could tell Jerry was uncomfortable and so was Donna. After all, Jillian was very confident and sure of herself. I guess that would bother some people. They met Jillian and really did not care for her. The following Monday at work, Jerry expressed his feelings about her. He felt that her attitude was poor and she would hold me back from succeeding in life. It caught me off guard. Jerry also felt she was "too good to be true." I did not feel that way about Jillian and I became angry with Jerry about his remarks. Jerry was a great role model and so was Donna. I thought about what Jerry had said later in the day and approached him.

I turned to him and said, "I thought about what you said but you are wrong about her."

Jerry said, "Maybe I am, we will soon find out. I'm just telling you as a friend to watch out. There's something about her that is not right. I just can't put my finger on it."

I said, "Jerry, you're too old to be jealous."

Jerry said, "James, I am not jealous. Look at my wife! Look at my life! You think I am jealous over her... now you're being silly."

I said, "I think you have been jealous for a while now."

Jerry said, "James, I love you like a son. I just want what's best for you. This girl isn't in it for love. Maybe she wants your money?"

I said, "Jerry, she has her own money. She works full time and brings home more than me. It can't be that!"

Jerry said, "Just give it some thought...it is all I am saying."

I sat there thinking about Jillian. We got along so well. First impressions were my mom loved her and so did the rest of the family. Especially the men... my uncles and brothers couldn't stop staring at her. I was trying to have an open mind about what Jerry was saying. He was the only one to not look at her like the others. I felt I was following my heart. I just didn't see what he had seen about her. I thought she was so sweet and had a heart of gold. Was I falling head over heels in love? My heart was being challenged like never before. I decided to listen to my heart for now. If I was wrong I felt it wasn't too late to get out...

## Chapter Eight

# Jillian

Over the next couple of years I tried to balance things out by spending more time at work, trying to make a living and stay ahead in my bills. I was not spending the time on my research like I should have done either. The relationship between Jerry and Jillian got darker and finally they were not speaking to one another. Jerry actually got to a point where he just despised her name. He became upset with me and was disappointed in me for choosing a woman like that. I still at this point did not see what he saw.

I said, "Actions speak louder than words in my life. Jillian has never showed me anything negative at any point. She seemed to love me for who I was and showed me she did. She showed me more than most, Jerry!"

Jerry said, "Don't bring her around here no more. Donna doesn't like her either. Dammit, James, I know evil when I see it and I thought you did too!"

I said, "I know evil, Jerry! I have been dealing with it my whole life…and that's fine, if that's what you want you got it. Just remember, Jerry, you chose it, not me!"

Calmly Jerry said, "That's right, I did."

I stared at him for a moment and finally walked away from Jerry. I went to work. It was time to keep moving forward and that's what Jillian and I did. Jillian gave up her condo and we moved in an apartment together. We were trying to make the best of what we had…each other! The apartment was in Waterford and close to my parents' home. It was a large place but at least we did not have to mow grass and shovel snow. We both had very busy schedules. I finally met Jillian's parents and they seemed to be good people.

I did think it was odd it took so long to meet them, though. They lived in California in a town called Camarillo; it's just north of L.A. Jillian said they did not like to travel or have quests. Finally Jillian got them to come out to Michigan for a visit. They only stayed for one night and were flying home the next day. Mrs. Foster was a sweet old gal and Mr. Foster looked like an old prospector you would find in an old mine out west (Miner 49er). Neither one of them looked like Jillian. In fact it must have been a miracle to produce a beautiful child like Jillian by the looks of these two, if you know what I mean.

Jillian said, "Welcome to Michigan, Dad and Mom, I missed you…both. I hope your trip was okay?"

Mr. Foster said, "It was fine, we had a good trip."

Mrs. Foster said, "We had a great trip. It's so good to meet you finally. Jillian tells me you love her very much and take good care of her."

I smiled at the news and said, "It's all true. It's very nice to meet you both finally."

Mr. Foster said, "There ain't no place like home, son. Next time you guys come out ta Cali for a spell, although it's much cooler here in Michigan."

Mr. Foster spit onto the ground. Mrs. Foster smacked him in his arm. Jillian acted as if she was being tormented with their presence. I smiled at them all. I thought it was kind of funny, although it was awkward.

To change the subject I said, "This is awesome! I am looking forward to dinner tonight. My mom and stepdad are coming to join us as well. You guys are going to fit together like corned beef and Swiss cheese."

I thought that analogy was something the Fosters could relate to…

Mrs. Foster whispered to Mr. Foster, "I doubt that."

I couldn't believe my own ears. I wonder why they would say something like that, especially in front of us. As I went to say how rude and disrespectful they were, Jillian gave them a very serious look…one I had never seen her give before. They both put their heads down in shame. She also gave the worst greeting I have ever seen a child give their parents. I mean they barely hugged after not seeing each other for four years. Yes they were hillbillies, but they seemed somewhat okay to me.

Jillian said, "James, if you would excuse us we have some family business to discuss and take care of. Sweetie, we will catch up to you in a few hours."

I said, "That's fine, I will see you in a little while then."

They were gone for most of the day. Later that night we met my parents for dinner at the local family restaurant.

My stepdad Pete laughed at the sight of them. My mom smiled and did what my mom does…that is, to be nice to everyone.

Pete said, "Nice to meet you both."

My mom said, "It's very nice to meet you."

Mr. Foster took an instant liking to my mom and reached out to her for a hug. He hugged her for almost thirty seconds.

Pete said, "That's enough for now, get your own wife."

Mr. Foster laughed at him a little and said, "Well I have one she's right yonder, have a go at her."

Mrs. Foster stood there looking at Pete, expecting a hug.

Pete stood his ground and kindly said, "Who's hungry… Let's go eat!"

We all walked into the restaurant and sat down.

During dinner not much was said by the Fosters. Jillian and I did most of the talking. We talked about family and having a family of our own someday. We explained how we both wanted to be financially secure before raising a child. My mom and dad both liked our plan, but the Fosters seemed eager for Jillian to have a child right away. This seemed to bother my parents. Mom and Pete felt we were too young.

Mr. Foster said, "It's about time you give us a younging, maybe a granddaughter."

Mrs. Foster said, "It would be so nice to have an addition to the family. You know I have been wanting a granddaughter, Jillian."

My mom said, "What's the hurry... they have only been dating a short time...they both need to finish school."

Pete said, "School is important."

Mr. Foster spoke up a little louder and said, "Why back in my day we was having younging's early! I mean fifteen was legal. We didn't worry about money. We lived off of the land. These new laws are ridiculous. A man can't even fart without getting a ticket, damn laws! Now we are even forced to have insurance on our automobiles and our health! It's socialism I say, socialism! He's a dictator, not a president!"

Mrs. Foster said, "Whoever voted for that fool gets what they deserve, we're going back to the old ways!"

Mr. Foster said, "Now, Mother, calm down. You know your heart."

We all sat there staring at the Fosters. I bet my parents were shitting up their backs because they voted for him. I looked at my mom and Pete and they both had "this dinner is over" looks on their faces.

Slightly embarrassed Jillian said, "Mom, Dad, we live in a civilized country now. James and I are going to do what's best for us, isn't that right, sweetie?"

I nodded yes to her and then said, "That's right, we are going to let things come natural. If a baby comes then it comes."

My mom slid me money and tucked it in between my leg and the seat.

My mom whispered, "That's for condoms, sweetie."

I couldn't help but smile. My mom was so funny at times. Besides, I knew what she meant. I felt at this point in my life every man must live his own life and make his own decisions. I slid the money back to her and placed it into her hand. I carefully nodded "no" to her. The rest of dinner everyone was quiet. All you could hear was silverware hitting the china. It was very awkward. My mom and Pete ate very quickly and asked our waitress for the check.

Jillian said, "Mom, dinner is on us tonight."

I said, "For sure, Mom, Pete, you guys always pay, we will take care of it tonight. Thank you both for coming."

Pete said, "It was our pleasure."

Mom said, "Thank you for dinner. It was nice to meet you both."

Mrs. Foster said, "Same to you."

Mr. Foster stared at my parents as if he was offended. My parents stared back as if they were ready to throw down and fist-fight. Pete's fists were clenched tight. His bottom lip curled up over the top one. I could tell they were upset. After dinner was over, the Fosters drove back to their hotel and my parents headed home. Jillian and I walked into the apartment and the phone began to ring. *Ring! Ring! Ring! Ring!*

Jillian said, "Could you get that, I'm going to take a shower."

It was as if she knew who was calling. I walked over and picked up the phone and said, "Hello."

My mom said, "Oh, James, those are some strange people."

I listened for the shower to turn on as I said, "What do you mean, Mom?"

Mom said, "Pete and I find it strange that they are Jillian's real parents. I mean look at them and look at Jillian. She is so beautiful and they're…"

As quiet as I could I said, "They're hillbillies, Mom…hold on a second."

I still did not hear the shower start. So I walked out

to the patio and slid the door closed.

I whispered, "Okay, I'm back."

Mom said, "It does look like they just climbed out from under a rock. Oh, James, there's something seriously wrong with the whole picture. I can't explain it but there is something seriously wrong. You be careful, Son."

I said, "It's funny you say that. Jerry and Donna felt the same way about her. In fact none of my friends want to be around her either."

Mom said, "My whole life my friends have been jealous of my looks and it has brought me to make some tough decisions on whom to trust. That is something Jillian and I have talked about. What I am saying is for you to trust your heart and have the courage to listen to it. Good friends are hard to come by, James."

Right away I thought about Jesus and how his friends treated him. They were there for him when things were going great. As soon as it got tough they bailed on him. For now I felt I was on the right path. One day at a time is all I have anyways.

I said, "I know, Mom… we have talked about this many times before. I can't speak for my friends. I can't control what they do either. Right now I think I'm on the right path. Until Jillian proves me wrong I am going to stay on this course."

Mom said, "She is such a beautiful girl and seems

like she has a good head on her shoulders. You have my blessing, James, to marry her if that's what you choose. I am trying to be supportive."

I said, "Thank you, Mom, it means a lot to me for you to say that. Jillian will be happy to hear that as well."

Mom said, "Pete said 'thank you for dinner' and gives his blessing as well."

I said, "That's great; tell him I said 'thank you.' You guys have a good night, I need to get to bed."

Mom said, "Good night, sweetie."

I said, "Good night, Mom."

As time flew by with work, friends, Jillian, and my studies, I found little time for myself or to write. Time flies when you're having fun! A few years later Jillian became pregnant. Eight weeks prior to her telling me the sex was so, so, so, hot…as I lay there on top of her hugging her tight and trying to catch up to my breath, something inside of me just knew it just happened. Jillian was so cute the way she told me. She came home from work and walked into the apartment. She set her purse down and then her book bag and walked up to me.

I said, "Hi, Jillian, how was your day?"

Jillian smiled and then hugged me and whispered, "James, how do you feel about having a beautiful baby girl in our family?"

I said, "What are you saying?"

Jillian whispered, "I am pregnant, James."

I said, "That's awesome…we are going to have a baby!"

Jillian said, "We are, and I just know it's going to be a girl. I can feel it."

I hugged her tight and said, "You make me so happy. I can't wait to share the news."

Jillian said, "They cannot determine the sex yet because it's too early, but I just know!"

I said, "I am happy either way."

Jillian said, "We must get married before she is born. That is a must, James."

I said, "Okay, let's get started making the arrangements then."

First things first, I did what I thought was not only the right thing but the honorable thing to do. I was going to ask her to marry me. I needed a perfect place to do it, so I went to work in hopes of setting up the perfect plan. This is what I did…

First after work I went to the local jewelers and picked out the perfect ring. Not too large but the perfect size that says "I appreciate you and love you very much." It was a 2.1 ct diamond ring set in white gold. It also had almost 2.0 ct in smaller stones scattered all over. It was so beautiful. I just knew it would speak volumes. From there I went to the restaurant where we had our very first date and asked for help. They were great and were very helpful. I then went to work and asked Jerry if he could arrange to borrow the old Corvette I was driving on our first date. Remember the side-piped Corvette? Jerry made it happen for me although he was not happy when I told him why, but he still came through.

Next I was off to set up the trip for our honeymoon. It was going to be great, I thought. At this point everything seemed to be going well with Jillian. Sex was awesome...I loved her...we got along well. We were saving money and our future seemed bright.

On Friday when I came home, Jillian was not home yet so I hid the Corvette over in the next parking lot parked in between two trucks. Then I watched for her closely out of the window to come home. When she arrived I called the restaurant to let them know we were coming soon. Jillian walked into the apartment.

I said, "Hey, you ready for dinner?"

Jillian said, "I will be in a few minutes."

She kissed me and walked into the bathroom to freshen up...

I don't understand women sometimes. My question is, "If you are naturally beautiful what on earth do you need makeup for? God made you the way you are...that's beautiful!"

I said, "Your transportation is waiting for you. I

will see you out front."

Jillian said, "There was not a car in your spot. Where did you park? I did not think you were home yet."

I winked and then said, "I will see you out front."

I walked over to the next parking lot and started it up. I felt Jillian did not care for the old car much, but that was not the point. It was time to take her back to day one! I drove over to our building and there she was standing on the sidewalk. When I stopped in front of her, she was shaking her head back and forth with a smile on her face. I turned the car off and got out to help her get in as I did before.

I said, "We are going to have fun tonight."

She was all smiles. I held out my hand to her. Jillian reached out and held my hand tight. I opened the car door and helped her get inside. I shut the door and walked around to the other side and got in. When I started up the car, it was so loud. The car shook as the pipes rumbled!

Jillian yelled, "Our first date was incredible."

I said, "It was. Try to relax… I know you had a rough day."

I let out the clutch and squealed the tires a little bit. I looked over at Jillian and she had an encouraged smile. When I drove onto M-59 I relived the moment we'd shared years ago. I took off as fast as the old car would go. When I let out the clutch in second gear,

Jillian slid back into her seat and reached for something to hold onto. The car kicked to the right and then quickly straightened out as the tires gained traction. Smoke filled the road. Burnt rubber filled our air space. When I shifted into third, it kicked to the left a little. I reached for the window switch and rolled the windows down to get fresh air. We both coughed a little from the smoke. The car was so loud and shook as we sped off to the restaurant. Although Jillian did not like speed much, she had a smile on her face from ear to ear. Jillian yelled, "That was awesome!"

I did not say a word. I just nodded my head. When we arrived, the valet parking person helped her out of the car using the same mat as before, covering the car's side pipe.

As she climbed out he said, "Careful now, ma'am."

As Jillian stood up she said, "Thank you!"

I handed the other valet person the keys with a huge smile on my face and said, "Be careful with second gear, it's lethal."

The valet person said, "No problem, sir."

We walked inside and the greeter immediately took us to our table we'd sat at years before. What was different was they closed off that section while we were there so we could have some privacy. They had put some red roses on the table in a beautiful vase. They hung red streamers from corner to corner and lowered the lighting. Many red and white candles filled the room; it seemed like a couple hundred at least. Some were placed on our table along with a bottle of orange juice in place of wine or champagne…as requested by me. They set up the table with the traditional seven-course dinner setting. When I looked back, just about everyone in the restaurant was looking through every peek hole they could find. I did not say a word. Neither did Jillian. We sat down and began to look at the menus.

A few minutes later the waitress came out and said, "Hello, I am Krista and I will be taking care of you both tonight. Do we know what we want?"

Jillian said, "I am starving, what are you having?"

As I folded my menu closed I said, "Steak and crab legs dinner, and you?"

Jillian said, "I want the steak special dinner."

The waitress said, "Great choices, I'll be back with drinks!"

Jillian whispered, "What do you think she meant by taking care of both of you tonight?"

I smiled at her and whispered, "Not what you're thinking."

Jillian giggled a little and whispered, "This is beautiful, James. Thank you for this."

I said, "You deserve it."

I knew she knew that I was going to ask her to

marry me. I looked around the restaurant at all of the people. I felt like a celebrity a little. Jillian stared at me while I was watching them. I felt as if they had tickets and were waiting to see the show. I felt it was the right time so I slid out the ring box and placed it on the table. Jillian stared at it with a huge smile on her face.

I said, "Inside that box is the key to my heart. If you choose to take it and be a part of my journey through life, I want you to know that I love you for you. It's not about money or what you own. It's about how you have treated me this far and how you showed me you love me for me. If you take it I promise to be the best husband you will ever come across on this planet. I will be the best dad that I can as well. One day at a time with that but I will give it my best."

Jillian began to cry and whispered, "James, I want that box more than you could imagine. I can't put into words how bad...I know you love me and I do love you for you. You have the best heart out of any-one I know."

Jillian continued to cry and she placed her arms on top of the table, reaching out to me. I reached out and touched hers. She looked at me and then back to the box. Her hands began to shake; her nerves were going out of control. She let go of my hand and slowly reached for the box. She gently picked it up and slowly opened it up. Tears dripped down her face right along with her makeup. Her eyes lit up with life as she pulled the ring from the box. She slid the ring onto her hand and stared at it, totally embracing the moment. You could hear "aww"s from the people in the restaurant as they waited for her to say yes. Jillian stood up and walked over to me.

She reached for my hand and pulled me up to her, hugging me very tightly. I hugged her back so tight as well.

Jillian whispered, "Yes, I will marry you."

Someone from the crowd yelled, "Come on, you're killing us here!"

I yelled, "She said 'yes'!"

Everyone began to clap and clap hard. We held onto one another and danced to our own music as if we were alone. The claps slowly stopped.

After a few minutes a woman yelled, "Congratulations, you guys!"

Jillian waved as we danced and softly said, "Thank you, everyone."

After a few minutes everyone settled down and went about their own business. We sat back down at the table and began to talk about our life together. We talked about baby names and the things we thought we might need for the baby. Our dinner came out and was delicious. Bite after bite we stared at one another. Over and over Jillian said how much she loved the ring and complimented my choice. The ring on her hand was so beautiful and it fit her perfectly.

When we were ready to leave I asked for the bill.

The waitress said, "It is on us, you guys. Thank you for sharing your beautiful moment with us. You had us all crying, including the boss, Gary."

At the same time we both said, "Thank you."

The waitress said, "Good luck to you both."

I said, "Thank you."

Jillian said, "Thank you and tell Gary 'thank you,' please."

The waitress said, "I will. God you guys look so good together."

Jillian said, "Thank you so much."

The date wasn't over just yet. We climbed back into the car and headed to a special location. I had a realtor friend hook us up with a million-dollar home in West Bloomfield that was for sale and was going through some renovations. It was completely empty except for Steve, whom they'd hired to look after the place until it sold. It was a very large home with seven master suites and all the trimmings one could hope for. It had a built-in pool and hot tub in the lower level. Half of the pool was outside and the other half inside. There was a large door that opened for the warmer weather. On the way there, Jillian must have asked me where we were going several times.

I kept smiling and said, "It's a surprise."

When we arrived there, my friend Steve was at the front door waiting for us as promised. He was our butler for the evening. The plan was for one night, Jillian and I were going to pretend to be wealthy beyond our dreams.

Jillian said, "What is this?"

I said, "Our home for tonight."

Jillian said, "Shut up!"

I said, "No really…it's Steve's gift to us."

Jillian said, "James, you never stop surprising me."

As I got out of the car Butler Steve said, "Welcome home, sir!"

I went with it and said, "It's always good to be home, Steven. Everything is in place?"

Steve said, "It is, sir."

I said, "Very good, my man."

I opened the door for Jillian and helped her out.

Jillian said, "Hello!"

Steve smiled and said, "Welcome home, madam."

Jillian said, "It's good to be home."

As Steve began to walk to his car he said, "Enjoy, buddy! You must be out by 7 A.M. The painting contractors will be here then to get started. Don't let me down, okay? The code to the door is the address if you get locked out."

I said, "No worries…no problem, we will be long

gone by then."

Steve opened the door to his BMW and said, "I set up a special spot for you both downstairs. Congratulations to you both…it's very nice to meet you finally, Jillian. Have fun, kids!"

Jillian said, "Nice to meet you as well."

Steve said, "We'll be in touch."

Steve was always in a hurry. I was so grateful for his help to make our night special. When we walked into the house, it was so cool inside. Whoever lived there before had great taste in decorating. It had several gorgeous diamond chandeliers inside. I thought the home was a cross between country and contemporary with a hint of elegant. Anyways, it was sweet and ours for the evening! We made our way through the house and finally went downstairs.

My phone began to vibrate and the notification tone said, "Hump day, yeah!"

Jillian giggled a little. It was one of her favorite commercials. Anyways, it was a text from Steve. The text read…*She is smoking hot how did you bag one like that?* I handed it to Jillian to read. She read it and just laughed and handed me the phone back. When we got downstairs, Steve had set up a blow-up bed and some juice and water for us to enjoy. There was a backpack sitting on the bed. He thought of everything, including a stack of towels and thick warm robes for us.

I pulled off my shirt and walked over and turned the lights off. It was dark at first until my eyes adjusted. The moonlight lit up the pool and spa. Jillian began to take her clothes off as I took off mine. For a moment we stood there staring at each other. We were swimming naked. I reached out for her. She reached out for me. When our hands met in the dark, not another word was spoken. That evening we made love many times. We swam and enjoyed each other's company. It truly was the perfect day.

During her pregnancy things took a horrible turn. I did not know what to think or do, so I went to my friend Steve for advice. Steve was not much help at all so that night I called for God. God did not respond. I was confused so I did what I thought was best. Jillian and I had set a wedding date to be wed in the fall. She wanted to be married by the ocean somewhere in the South. As I told my family of the news, they seemed somewhat disappointed.

Mom said, "It's best to slow down and take one thing at a time."

I said, "Mom, she is pregnant, and is due in the spring. What else am I supposed to do? I feel it's best."

Mom said, "James, I am so happy for you. I guess follow your heart. That's what I taught you to do."

My mom became very excited and seemed to look past the wedding. All she could think about was the grandbaby. The rest of my family seemed disappointed and felt I should give it some serious thought before I married her. Jason especially did not care for her either. He had kept his distance. Through the summer, Jillian became very distant and secretive. Our conversations were short and directly to the point. She began spending money hand over fist and soon our savings disappeared just like that with nothing to show for it. I had kept that a secret from my family. I was embarrassed about it. My relationship with Jerry seemed to come to a close so I decided to look for another job. Just before I told Jerry I'd found a new job, he tried one last time to get me to see the light with Jillian. I finally told him the news of the pregnancy and my marriage proposal to her. Jerry became frustrated with me and told me I was out of my mind.

Jerry said, "James, you do not have to marry this woman to be a father to that child!"

I said, "Jerry, where is the honor in that?"

Jerry stood his ground and did not say another word. The next day and still angry with Jerry, I told him I'd found a new job and that I was giving him my two weeks' notice. Jerry became angry and let me go that day. I took a job at the local auto dealership selling used cars. I decided to follow through with the wedding, ignoring everyone's warnings. That night I thought about God and turned to speak with him to get help again, but he never responded to my cry. I begged for assistance but was ignored. The only thing I could do was to continue to follow my heart and do the honorable thing until something changed. All I could think about was the baby and looking after him or her. Life as I knew it became extremely stressful.

That fall the wedding date arrived and I was standing at the altar, in the park next to the ocean in Myrtle Beach.

The woman priest pulled me aside and said, "Let's take a walk, James. We will be right back."

Jillian said, "Don't be gone long, okay?"

I said, "We won't."

As we walked she said, "It's my duty to God and to you to point out to you that you seem so distant and unsettled. To me you don't look like a man that wants to truly get married."

I said, "I am confused, that's for sure."

As we walked, I explained to the priest in a very short story of the situation.

I said, "She is pregnant and I do love her. But something is different now. I don't know if it's because of the pregnancy or what. I can't put my finger on it."

The priest said, "James, that's very noble but in the end whose heart are you following… yours or hers?"

I walked for a minute and finally said, "Mine, I think… I am confused but I feel this is the right thing to do."

The priest said, "Very well then, if that's how you feel we will proceed with the wedding. You have come a long ways to be wed. Maybe it is just nerves."

I said, "Yeah maybe."

We walked back to the park.

Jillian said, "Everything okay?"

I said, "It is."

Jillian said, "James, it's just nerves, I know you well. It's just nerves."

I said, "You're probably right."

Jillian smiled at me and turned to the priest and said, "Please proceed."

As I stood there listening to the wedding vows, I could feel my heart sing a new song and I chose to ignore it. It was so powerful…almost overwhelming. Something inside of me wanted to grab the license and rip it up and run. At the same time, all I could think about was the baby. What was I going to do? I began to sweat…my part was coming fast…

I said, "I do."

The priest said, "From the power invested in me from God and the states of North and South Carolina, you are now man and wife. Congratulations to you both."

Jillian looked at me and gave me a short kiss and said, "James you made me the happiest woman on the planet."

I smiled at Jillian because I did not know what to say. My heart continued to yell out, "Rip it up and run while you still can!" We thanked the priest for her time and gave her a donation to the church. I paid the photographer. We gathered our things and went back to the hotel so Jillian could get some rest. While she was sleeping, I went down to the restaurant to get some food. I felt like a total fool and a coward. I sat at the bar waiting for my food thinking, why couldn't I say no?

I said, "Bartender, could I have a shot of Wild Turkey please?"

The bartender said, "Coming right up!"

I sat there sipping on my shot thinking...Yes, Jillian is beautiful...when we make love...wow... but what was it about her? Was Jerry right this whole time? Was Jillian the devil in disguise?

When we returned home, Jillian continued to be a big disappointment. I would tell her to quit spending money that we didn't have. She would say "okay" but would go out behind my back and get another credit card and run it up. Before I knew it, banks were calling me asking me where their money was. I became angry with her and kept my distance from her. I finally took control over the finances. After a while and a few awesome months selling cars, I quickly turned things around and got enough money together to pay off our bills and purchase a home. It wasn't much but it was a start. I made up my mind to stay with her and raise our baby together. I did not want any of my children to come from a broken family like mine.

Jillian's water had broken and we raced to the hospital! I was so excited to be a dad. When we arrived at the hospital, I pulled up in front of the E.R. entrance. I ran around to the other side of the car to get Jillian out! At that point a nurse came running out to help with a wheelchair. Jillian stood up on her own power and began to walk.

I said, "She is having a baby!"

The nurse said, "That's awesome, my first E.R. baby!"

Jillian said, "We have a room reserved upstairs in the birthing center, a LDRP room."

The nurse said, "Okay, sweetie, we will get you there."

As we approached the desk, the desk nurse said, "Name, please."

Jillian said, "Martin."

The desk nurse looked at the computer screen and said, "Take her upstairs and we will notify the doctor you're here, Nurse Room 5 please."

Jillian said, "Thank you."

The desk nurse said, "Good luck, Martins!"

I said, "Thank you."

She helped put Jillian in the wheelchair and started pushing her to the elevators.

Jillian said, "She is coming today."

The nurse said, "You already know the sex?"

Jillian said, "No, we both wanted to be surprised. I just know it's a baby girl though."

The nurse said, "How about you, Dad?"

I said, "I…it makes no difference to me. I am just excited to be a dad."

Sarcastically the nurse said, "Come on now, don't be modest… you are wanting a son, right?"

I looked at her in the eyes and with a hint of feeling disrespected said, "Didn't you hear what I said?"

I began thinking to myself…is this lady for real or what? Shit…what an asshole! Who says these things to people?

The nurse said, "I didn't mean it to be a bad thing or mean to disrespect you. Most men want a son is all."

I said, "I am not most men."

Jillian said, "James, it's okay, she doesn't know you and she is assuming you're like most men. Which are pigs by the way? Nurse, James is an exception to the rule. You would think God made an exact mold of himself when you refer to James. James is perfect!"

The nurse looked up at me and smiled. I rolled my eyes and looked at Jillian.

I said, "I am far from perfect."

Jillian said, "Not in the eyes of God."

I smiled at her and the nurse. The nurse waited for the doors to the elevator to open and pushed Jillian inside. We all got inside the elevator and headed to the 5th-floor birthing rooms.

I said, "Our doctor is coming?"

The nurse said, "I am sure he will be there in time. Try to relax, Mr. Martin."

I said, "Thank you."

The doors dinged and began to open. The nurse pushed her out into the hallway and headed to room 5. I followed closely behind. When we arrived at room 5, Jillian got out and began to undress.

The nurse said, "Let's get you comfy."

She helped Jillian onto the bed and gave her a robe to cover up with and a warm blanket. Another nurse came into the room and checked to see if Jillian was dilated enough to give birth. She put on a rubber glove and inserted her hand into Jillian's vagina.

She said, "4 cm not quite there yet. I'll be back, honey, try and rest if you can; it's going to be a long night."

Jillian said, "What do you mean long night? She is coming soon. Get my doctor here now!"

I said, "Try to relax. I'll keep track of the doc."

Jillian said, "I love you, James."

I said, "I love you. Do you want me to do anything for you…rub your back or neck?"

Jillian let out a little cry as she began to have another contraction.

I stood next to her and said, "Remember the breathing. Let's get started!"

Jillian took a deep breath and slowly let it out. Several hours had past. As the contractions got closer, the stress level in the room went through the roof. Jillian began calling me names...things I never heard her say before...in a language I'd never heard before. It was as if it was almost biblical, I felt.

I looked at her funny and said, "What are you saying?"

Jillian looked at me as if she wanted to kill me and yelled, "You did this to me, you bastard! I am going to get you for this, James Martin!"

She began breathing really fast! I held her hand tight and wiped away sweat off of her forehead.

She screamed out so loud, "AWWWWWWWWWW SON OF A BITCH!"

The pain must have been near unbearable, I felt.

The doctor walked into the room and said, "I am here, Jillian, please calm down....do your breathing. I need to check to see if you are at 10 cm yet."

Jillian did not cut the doctor any slack either when she said, "Finally you're fucking here! Get this kid out of me!"

I said, "Welcome aboard, doc!"

He smiled at me and then snapped on a rubber

glove and checked her for the dilation. A couple more nurses came into the room.

I said, "Your breathing, you need to do the breathing we learned!"

Doc said, "Okay we are there, let's start pushing."

Jillian yelled, "Finally for fuck's sake! Grrrrrrr!"

She pushed so hard! She screamed at the top of her lungs as she continued to push! Her face turned so red.

After thirty seconds I yelled, "Breathe, girl, breathe!"

Jillian stopped pushing and began to do the breathing. In short breaths she continued.

Doc said, "Push again! One more time! I see the baby's head!"

And just like that our baby came sliding out into the doctor's hands.

Doc set the baby down and said, "It's a beautiful baby girl."

She began to cry as Doc cleaned out her mouth and clamped off the umbilical cord. The nursing staff took the baby and began to clean her up.

I stood there holding Jillian's hand and whispered to her, "It's all over now. I am so proud of you."

Jillian said, "I am proud of you. Look at our baby girl, she is so beautiful."

The nurse said, "Are you ready to hold her, Mama."

Jillian said, "Of course."

I watched as Jillian took her baby girl for the first time. The look of *joy* on Jillian's face filled the room's atmosphere. The doctor left the room along with most of the nurses.

The nurse said, "In a few minutes we will take baby to the nursery. Did you guys have a name yet?"

Jillian looked at me and said, "Well, Daddy?"

I said, "Abigail Jane Martin is her name."

Jillian said, "Is it okay if Dad feeds her first? He wants to have a talk with her."

I looked at Jillian. It was as if she could read my mind. Jillian looked deep into my eyes.

The nurse said, "Absolutely, you're using formula then?"

Jillian said, "Yes."

She broke eye contact with me and closed her eyes. The nurse came with a portable table called a baby transport and took Abigail to the nursery. They kicked me out of the room to finish up with Jillian.

I kissed her and whispered, "I love you."

Jillian whispered, "I love you. Take good care of our baby girl, James."

I said, "I am on it."

I walked out of the room and ran to catch up with my new baby girl. She looked so content all wrapped up in the blankets. When we arrived at the nursery, I sat down in a rocking chair and watched the nurse finish checking her in. She came over to me and put a pink matching bracelet on my wrist. She reached into the transport and picked up Abigail and set her down in my arms.

I whispered, "There you are, little girl…I got you, Daddy's got you."

Abigail began to fuss a little as our eyes met for the first time.

I whispered, "Shhhh, Dad has you. You are safe with me. It's all right, Abigail, it's alright, Daddy's got you. Look, we have pink matching bracelets."

I held up mine so she could see it. Abigail took a deep breath and closed her eyes. I began to talk to her while she slept. After my daughter was born (baby Abigail, just love her so much), things seemed to take a little turn towards the better. Jillian seemed to go back to the way she was when we met. I figured what she was going through had to be because of the pregnancy. It was hard to forget she almost broke us financially. Jillian and I became a little closer and began to spend more time together, making the best of the situation. She went back to work and got herself back in shape.

Many nights I wondered where God was. I missed speaking to him and decided to spend more time on my research. It was going quite well. When Abigail slept, so did Dad. When she napped during the day, I read as much as I could. Six months later God came to me...

God said, "James, I am disappointed in you. Why did you marry this Jillian? She is not your soul mate!"

I said, "I followed my heart, I thought."

God said, "When the priest told you to think about it and listen to your heart, why didn't you listen? You know what your heart said. It said do not marry this woman, it's wrong. It also said rip up the license and run away! I have a woman for you, James, for you to love and spend the rest of your life with. You were not ready for marriage yet. You must complete your research first."

I got mad and said, "I want to have a life of my own! Is that too much to ask for! I chose to marry her and it will work out!"

God said, "James, I understand why you are angry, nobody wants to admit their mistakes. I too want you to have a life of your own, just not with her!

I need you to finish the book first!"

I said, "I do not think people care anymore about religion or going to church anymore! They feel like hope is lost! There is no sense in finishing a book I never started!"

God said, "James, you listen to me. You have a beautiful young daughter to look after now. Abigail is so precious; I heard your promise you made to me when she was born. I loved the way you held her and told her the promise. Let's not forget why I chose you. Now, once the girl is old enough to fend for herself you will finish the book."

I calmed down and said, "Okay, God; okay."

God said, "When she sleeps during the day, you do research and write."

I said, "Okay."

God said, "By the way, James; Jillian is not who you think she is. I put you to the test so you would know what I mean when I say follow your heart! What is done is done now. Stay with your daughter, but watch out for that woman."

I said, "Okay."

It got quiet for a moment and then God said, "It will be a while before we speak again. Work hard on the research, James, and help me give hope back to the world…I can't stress to you how important this book will be to mankind someday. You will be a legend that no person will ever forget."

I said, "A legend is for heroes, God, not me…not James Martin. I am nobody special. I am just a man."

God said, "A great man and a great person. You will see, James; have faith in me and I will continue to have faith in you. Also, do not forget why church is so important to mankind. A place to worship their God is important to the soul. It gives the mind and soul a sense of belonging and gives people a place to confess their sins. It's a place they can go to leave their troubles behind. Do not forget to add this to your book; write it word for word as I just spoke it."

I began to write down God's words and said, "Okay I got it, I wouldn't forget."

God said, "Good luck, James, I believe in you. Don't forget you are only here one time. Make the most of it."

I said, "Okay."

When I woke up the next day, I had a whole new outlook in life. Raising Abigail became priority one. Watching out for my life was number two. I was able to encourage Jillian to go back to work full time and spend time keeping herself in shape at the local gym. I thought she seemed happiest when she looked her best. There was definitely something wrong; she was unhappy with herself and I didn't know what else to do that would inspire her. For now all I knew what to do was to keep a close eye on her. Talk about keeping your friends close and your enemies closer.

Abigail and I were having a blast. Being a dad was the best feeling in the world to me. Changing diapers was not so bad either, although some of them were unbearable. Sometimes doing chores around the house was tough. When I had to do something like mow the grass, I put Abigail in her car seat with a hat and sunglasses. I placed her on the picnic table on the patio that was in the shade. Each time I passed her by, I made funny faces to keep her laughing. She would giggle just about every time. I tried to make everything fun for her no matter what we did. Watching her grow was amazing and adorable. Did I say what her first word was? You guessed it... Dada! I felt like the best Dad in the whole world when she said it. To be completely honest, I spent the last month saying "dada" to her. I figured after she heard it a few thousand times I was a shoe-in? When Abigail began to walk, I couldn't get the video camera out fast enough. I tried to capture as much footage as I could. I took a lot of pictures as well. When Jillian came home at night, we would try to eat dinner together as a family. I would catch her up on that day's activity. Jillian seemed like she was trying to make it work. I suppose right now you are wondering why I married Jillian in the first place? I guess if I shared it with you, it would make more sense why we are together.

It's going to get warm in here...

See, our third date was amazing. As I said earlier, Jillian did things to me and made me feel safe and special like no other woman. With the other women before it was just sex. I was so young; I did not know what love was at the time. I fell in love with Jillian right away. She captured my whole heart. Jillian invited me over to her house to watch a movie. After the movie was over, we began to make out. We kissed and kissed some more. Our breathing got heavier and heavier. As we kissed, our passion got stronger and stronger. One piece of clothing at a time slid off as we slowly worked our way to the bedroom removing the rest of each other's clothes. I had no problems removing her bra either. I was well trained at this point. One-handed release!

Jillian whispered, "I am impressed."

As I helped remove her bra I whispered, "Just wait, there's more."

When her bra slid down revealing her breasts and nipples, my mouth began to water. I wanted them… I reached out to touch them. We slid down onto the bed. She was so sexy. I was all over her like a new silk shirt does when it touches your body. All I wanted was to please her. And I knew she wanted to please me.

We kept kissing so softly that we kept giving each other goose bumps all over. On occasion we would gently bite each other's tongues just to keep it fun. She began to go up further onto the bed. Her blonde hair shined in the moonlight as she slid herself up on the bed and laid her head on the pillows. I began to kiss the top of her foot and slowly worked my way up her leg. They were so sexy. I gently grazed her vagina and continued up her stomach. I kissed her chest and then up her neck, gently kissing her ears and then her lips again. Jillian reached for my penis and began to caress me slowly and gently. I reached down and touched her vagina and began to masturbate her. Jillian began to moan out loud as I penetrated her. Slowly I wanted to please her and feel her love. In and out I went with my finger.

I searched for that special spot she desired the most by listening to her moans. I quickly found it by the quick breaths she would take just before she moaned as I touched it again and again. I stayed focused on pleasing her. I wanted her to learn the true meaning of "multiple" in the dictionary. After a few minutes wetter and wetter she came. I could feel her tighten up as she began to have an orgasm. She let go of me and grabbed the sheets tightly and began to breathe heavily and started to sweat even more. Her vagina became very wet as she came. All I could think about was pleasing her again… She must cum again. I continued to masturbate her and hold her tight. I grabbed her from behind and hugged her with one hand and rubbed and masturbated her with the other. She was so wet…I caressed her breasts and kissed her neck and ear. I wanted her so badly…

In the sexiest voice I'd ever heard she whispered, "I can feel your hard cock on my ass. Fuck yes…that is exciting me…I am almost ready for it… keep going. I can feel the tip."

Jillian was breathing so hard. I just wanted to be inside of her.

I whispered, "Whenever you're ready."

She squeezed my penis so hard and held onto it. I wanted her in the worst way. It became all I could think about. I slid over to her side and began kissing her chest and licked away the salty sweat from her nipples. I desired her sweat as one would water out in the middle of a desert. There was something unique about her I wanted. I had to have her. She was like no other woman. I got aggressive and sucked on her nipples and continued to masturbate her. She continued to hold onto my penis tightly. She screamed out loud as she released her orgasm again.

"Awwwwwww…," Jillian whispered. "My turn…"

The way her mouth was open was sexy as hell as she took deep breaths… I continued to kiss her as she grabbed me and hugged me tight. Jillian sat up and pushed me onto my back. She flipped her hair back and reached for my penis and climbed on top of me… gently she guided my penis inside of her and slowly slid down on it. Deeper and deeper I went inside of her as she rode up and down on me some more. Jillian sat up and absorbed my full length…she cried out as she went all the way down.

"Mercy," she whispered.

Slowly she began to slide back and forth on me. She made me so horny and to desire her even more. All I wanted in the whole world was to make love with her and give her my seed. She was so wet and tight. She rocked slowly back and forth, moaning softly. Her moans were like a soft romantic song, something you would hear only in the heavens. I began to touch her all over… caress her…love her… she was so beautiful. After a few minutes I could feel her tighten up again. She began to rock faster and faster until she finally screamed out, releasing her orgasm again. I could feel my balls get soaked as she came. She fell to my chest, breathing so heavily. I hugged her tight and continued to make love to her slowly for a few minutes while she caught her breath. She slowly sat up and spun around so that her back was to me. She lay back onto my chest while I continued to make love to her.

She turned and softly whispered, "Do anything you want to me but anal."

I kissed her and turned her on her stomach. I reconnected with her and began to make love to her some more. It was gentle at first but I was eager to please her more. Jillian reached for a pillow and buried her face into it.

She whispered, "Harder."

I began to give it to her harder as she requested. I

felt she could read my mind.

She whispered, "Faster."

I began to go faster…

She said, "Harder!"

This was my dream come true…how did she know? I wondered. On each thrust I gave her all of my length. My legs began to slap her butt cheeks, I was pumping on her so hard. They were making a smacking sound with each thrust. Harder and harder I made love to her. I didn't want her to ever forget James Martin! We both began to sweat more and more, and Jillian began to moan louder and louder. As I held onto her hips I could feel my grip slip from her sweat. I held on tighter as I pumped my rock-hard penis into her. I could feel her tighten up and I desired to go faster and harder yet!

I began to feel my balls tingle with excitement as the sperm began to make its way out. I began to breathe so hard. Jillian must have felt the excitement as well because she seemed to tense up, expecting me to cum.

Jillian yelled, "I want it all!"

My head became so lightheaded. All I cared about was showing her how much she was loved and how much I loved loving her and pleasing her some more. Jillian screamed real loud as I released into her. Jillian was a screamer and that was that and I liked it!

Jillian yelled, "Fuck yes, don't you stop…keep going!"

I held onto her real tight as I filled her with cum. I never came so hard and so much with any other partners as I did with her. The next pump was almost as powerful as I released some more into her. I took a deep breath and grabbed her hips and pulled her onto me tight and held on for what seemed an eternity. Time stood still as my penis pumped my remaining seed into her! My head was spinning. I soon fell onto her back, causing her to fall to the bed. I lay there a minute, breathing so heavily. After a minute I broke our connection and lay next to her, kissing her back and neck. She soon turned and lay on my chest, listening to me breathe.

Jillian looked up at me in the eyes and took a deep breath and said, "That was the best sex ever. I mean it. My head is spinning I am so lightheaded right now. That is how beautiful babies are made! Get rest… we are going again."

I couldn't speak I was breathing so hard. I smiled at her. She stared into my eyes, smiling back. Our souls felt like they hugged and would not separate. I knew at that moment I would have to be with her forever no matter what. I kept smiling and hugged her while still trying to catch my breath. It wasn't just sex like the other times before. This woman captured my heart and danced with my soul. I could feel her love deep into me as she hugged me tight.

Now do you see why I am so passionate about her? Honestly ask yourself, would you be if you were I? Take a moment and think about it.

Jillian slowly turned things around between us. She began to work and work hard. One by one the credit cards disappeared and our savings went back up. She became obsessed with money practically overnight. It became a very strong passion for her to be wealthy. While she was at work I spent time with my other woman in my life: Abigail.

Abigail's hair began to grow and grow. Her curls turned into long locks and she looked even more adorable. When I ran around town picking up things for the house, women would see her and say how precious she was and ask to touch her hair. Abigail would say no to them sometimes. Other times she loved the attention. As she got older, she looked more and more like her mommy. I had a day off of work, so Abigail and I decided to go into the library to pick up some books to read. My computer at home quit working, but I needed to continue my research until the new one arrived. I found some books on Greek mythology and cryptography. It was time to continue working on God's book. Of all people to let down it was not going to be him, at least not on purpose.

When I returned home I got Abigail ready for bed and tucked her in for the night. Knowing Jillian was the enemy, I could not treat her poorly. She was the mother of my baby girl after all. Jillian was in the shower getting ready for bed when she called for me to come in there.

Jillian said, "Is Abby in bed?"

I said, "Yes, she is still awake though. How was your day?"

Jillian said, "I had an excellent day, and I got a bonus from the boss today.

It's right there on the counter."

I turned around and picked up the envelope. I lifted the flap and was amazed at the cash he had given her.

I said, "Wow, Jillian, what did you have to do to get this?"

Jillian got mad instantly with that remark.

She said, "I did not have relations with him if that's what you mean."

I said, "Why would you think that? I did not say that!"

Jillian rinsed her hair and reached for her towel. It made me mad that she would insinuate something like that. I set the cash down and walked into our bedroom. I was getting tired of her mood swings. I picked up one of the books from the library and began to read about secret codes. Jillian came in the room and began to apologize.

She sat down at the end of the bed and said, "I am sorry, okay! I am uptight with work and you know my boss is a male chauvinist pig."

I said, "I know he is, and I accept your apology."

Jillian said, "I outsold them all this month. That is where the cash is from."

I said, "That is awesome! You're doing well and I am proud of you."

I smiled at her. I flipped the book back up as she stood up to get dressed.

Jillian noticed the book and said, "What on earth would you, an auto sales professional, do with a book like that?"

I quickly lied and said, "I am thinking about using codes at work to instruct with, so customers do not get uptight when we talk about high numbers? People get stressed out buying expensive cars."

Jillian bought it, thank God! She checked on Abigail and came back into the room. She climbed into bed and shut down her light. I read for hours before I fell into a deep sleep. I woke up to the alarm going off. I had to get up and take Abigail to childcare. Once I got her loaded into the car, I ran back inside to get my books.

I gave sleepy Jillian a kiss good-bye and said, "You had better get up, you're going to be late.... Jillian, did you hear me?"

As I walked towards the hallway I heard a deep, dark, and very familiar voice say, "Do not worry, I will make it."

I stopped at the doorway and stood there facing the door. My worst fears came frightfully true at that very moment. My hair stood tall on my neck and all I could think about was to fight back. I slowly turned around, expecting the worst, and looked at Jillian. She looked at me with those black eyes and smiled. Darkness filled her soul and black-colored blood filled her veins. Slowly her eyes turned back to blue and her skin color returned to normal.

After a few minutes Jillian said, "What?"

She stared at me, confused. I snapped out of my trance I was in.

I said, "No... Nothing, talk to you later."

Jillian said, "Sweetie, have a good day. I will talk with you later."

I went out to the car and climbed in. I sat there thinking to myself...Nooo, it can't be! Not her...not Jillian. I remembered what God had said but the reality of it just hit home. At times I would forget she was the enemy, I loved her so much. My heart was crushed. All I could think about was Abigail and her safety.

Abigail said, "Daddy, are you alright? Did you forget what today is?"

I said, "No of course not, sweetie. Are you excited?"

Abigail nodded her head up and down a few times, smiling from ear to ear.

It was my turn to buy doughnuts for breakfast for the childcare. Abigail was going to pick out her first breakfast for everybody. She was extremely excited to say the least.

When we arrived at the doughnut store, Abigail stood at the counter looking at all of the different doughnuts.

The counterperson said, "Well now, aren't you a little young to be picking out doughnuts?"

Abigail said, "Well it's my turn to get breakfast for my friends at daycare and Mrs. Butler and Ms. Greene. I need to pick something they will like."

Abigail scanned back and forth looking for the right ones.

I said, "Pick some out so we can get going."

Abigail looked some more and finally said, "We would like thirty of the ones with frosting, please with the frosting and my daddy's going to pay for it."

Everyone in line that was listening to her giggled a little.

The counterperson pointed to a tray and said, "These?"

Abigail said, "Yes please. They sure look good!"

The counterperson said, "These are great! You

made a great choice for your friends. I'll bet you're going to be popular today, honey."

Abigail said, "I hope so. If not Dad and I are going to get fat."

Everyone began to giggle at her a little.

The counterperson smiled as she filled a couple of boxes up and said, "Thank you for coming today."

I handed her the money as Abigail said, "See you next month."

The counterperson said, "I am looking forward to it. Take care now."

I said, "Thank you."

Abigail said, "How did I do, Dad?"

I said, "You were perfect. You spoke right up and I am proud of you. I am kinda in a hurry today and I won't be able to stay for very long, so you let me know tonight how everything went, okay?"

Abigail said, "Okay, Daddy."

I took Abigail to childcare and brought in the doughnuts. I'd set them down on the table when Ms. Greene approached me.

Ms. Greene said, "Hi, Mr. Martin, thank you for sharing today. How are you today, Abby?"

Abigail said, "I am doing well. We had fun picking them out."

I said, "How are you, Ms. Greene?"

Ms. Greene was looking at the doughnuts and said,

"Well, thanks. These look great. Nice choice, let's get the drinks, okay?"

Abigail said, "Good-bye, Daddy. Talk with you later tonight."

I reached down and gave her a kiss and a hug and said, "Have fun today."

Abigail walked away to be with her friends.

Ms. Greene said, "Mr. Martin, thanks again for the breakfast."

I said, "No problem. Good day to you."

I walked out to the car and headed to work. As I drove out to the road, I spotted Jillian's car a few parking spaces down. I didn't see her in it. I looked around and did not see her. Just as I decided to stop, she sat up in the seat and pulled out and drove away in the opposite direction.

I said, "What in hell is she doing?"

I decided it was time to hide my notes elsewhere instead of under the seat in my car. I just needed a good spot. Somewhere safe...

I began to think out loud and said, "Nowhere is safe. I have most of them memorized anyways. I will burn them..." I drove on the dirt roads on my way to work and pulled over. In a panic I began searching the car for matches and none were to be found. I checked every compartment and crack in the seats. I opened the ashtray and pushed in the lighter. I grabbed one piece of my notes and waited for the thing to pop out.

I yelled, "Come on, you stupid thing."

*Pop!* I pulled out the lighter, staring at it and my note written in God's words. I quickly reread it one last time and pushed the lighter into the corner. It slowly began to burn. I opened the door and walked to the back of the car. I made a pile out of all the notes. I sat down and began to read them one by one until I felt it was safe to burn it. Then I tossed it into the burn pile. I felt in my heart that it was the right thing to do. Let's just hope when it was time I could remember them. As they burned I got up to get a stick to stoke the fire with. I stood there pushing the notes around, watching them go up into flames. After a few minutes the fire started to go out. I waited until there was only ashes left and kicked dirt on them.

When I got to work, I unloaded the books at my desk and went into the morning meeting. Later that day I did not hear from Jillian like I usually did. I immediately thought about what God had said about her. That she is not who I think she is. Who is she then? I thought. After this crazy morning I knew it was time to take action. I know I said this once already, but I am saying it again. Keep your friends close and your enemies closer. This worked well in my case, at least I thought for now. The more I thought about Jillian, the weirder it got. She has no friends; no family; her mom and dad never come around anymore. They are always too busy digging for gold, I guess?

When I mentioned my friends she would always say, "I am tired; can't it be just you and me?"

On my way home after picking up Abigail, I thought about what God said again. "She is not who you think she is." Who is she then? It was time to ask her. My plan was simple: it's Friday and I am going to get her drunk! I never had seen her drink much of anything, so I did not know what to get her. I stopped at the party store on the corner and walked inside with Abigail. I walked up to the counter and asked for a few bottles of everything. I told the woman behind the counter I was having a party and needed some assistance if she had any ideas for mixing drinks that taste good. She gave me a book on being the best instant bartender. I took it and my new bottles of booze home.

Jillian was running late as usual, so I decided to get Abigail ready for bed. She went to sleep just before Jillian came home. I heard the car door shut. At that moment I decided not to ask her about that morning. There was nothing I could do about it anyways. I knew God had my back. I was not going to give up on faith. Besides, I was more interested in who she really was. When she walked into the house, she looked as beautiful as she did on our first date…she was captivating.

I said, "Hello, gorgeous!"

Jillian said, "Why hello, handsome!"

She began to remove her clothes to go get in the shower.

I said, "Not so fast."

She put her small suit coat back on.

She said, "What's going on?"

I said, "Right this way, please."

I escorted her to the makeshift bar I had made up in the kitchen. Jillian sat down on the barstool I pulled out for her.

I said, "What can I get for you?"

Jillian said, "One James, please?"

I said, "I am sorry, we are all out of James tonight, ma'am; what else?"

Jillian said, "James, you know I do not drink."

I said, "I know this about you, but it's time to let our hair down, sort of speaking. So what are you going to have?"

Jillian said, "Okay, I see you are not going to let this go. I will have a gin and tonic, please."

I pulled out my trusty book and went to work. I topped it off with a lime wedge and slid it over to her.

Jillian said, "I am impressed. Next time make it a 50/50 drink, please."

I quickly inserted the straw I forgot and said, "I will do that. Enjoy!"

Jillian said, "All right, what's all of this about?"

I said, "I wanted to do something different tonight, and this is what I wanted to do."

Jillian said, "We have great sex all of the time so that can't be what this is about."

I said, "Stop worrying and relax. It's me... remember?"

Jillian sipped on her drink and we moved to the couch to be more comfortable. Jillian kicked off her shoes and we began to talk about life. The more she talked, the more I realized she was just misunderstood by most people. I did not forget what God said, though. Being misunderstood was something we both shared in common. Jillian finished her drink and I got up to make another for her. As the night progressed, Jillian became very relaxed and loosened up. After several drinks I asked her what she saw in me.

I said, "Why did you pick poor little James Martin when you could have had any man you wanted?"

Jillian sat there for a minute all drunk and said, "Can't a girl have the best man she can? I don't know, James; I loved you the first time I laid eyes on you. Is that a crime?"

I said, "No, not at all."

Jillian said, "Besides, when I saw you, I knew you would make beautiful babies, and drinks too!"

She handed me her glass, giggling.

Jillian said, "One more, please!"

I smiled because it was true. Abigail was beautiful. I took Jillian's glass and made her another drink. I walked back in the living room and handed it to her. Jillian smiled at me and patted the seat next to her, wanting me to sit there. I sat by her and stared into her soft blue eyes. I did not forget what I saw that day. But I still did not see what God or anyone else could see when she was normal. I felt as if Jillian was misunderstood, like I said earlier. I decided to give her the benefit of the doubt until she proved me wrong. I know love is blind, but I do not have all the answers either. Besides, Jillian and I had an interesting relationship. I can honestly say it was never boring. Jillian sipped her drink and continued to look into my eyes.

Jillian said, "James, why are you doing all of this research all of the time? Are you trying to write a book or something?"

I was not sure if she was just throwing that out there or if she knew what was asked of me. I'd never told a soul.

I said, "I just enjoy reading and educating myself. I can learn more in the library than any person could by going to the best of schools in the world. I can honestly say I've learned more than most will ever achieve."

Jillian said, "You did not answer my question, are you writing a book?"

Instead of lying I answered her with a question.

I said, "What would give you that idea?"

Jillian sat there staring at me with her beautiful smile and said, "I think writing a book is the greatest goal any educated man could achieve in life. What a great milestone."

I said, "I will have to remember that, Jillian."

Jillian held up her glass high and said, "Here's to making beautiful babies!"

I held my glass to hers and said, "Cheers to that."

I sat there looking at Jillian with my head rested on the back of the sofa.

Jillian laid her head close to mine and said, "Don't worry, James, everything is going to turn out as it should."

I smiled at her and said, "I know it will."

I decided it did not matter who she truly was. What mattered was she was loyal to me and Abigail and that was all that mattered. Until that changed, we stay the course and make the best of it. We all have a past. My past was not good either. I was not proud of my parents and my childhood, although we all have to start somewhere. I stood up and walked over to the stereo to play some soft music. I set my drink down and reached for Jillian's hand. Jillian smiled and sat her drink down and walked over to me. We began to dance and hold each other like a married couple should. At times Jillian seemed to be the perfect wife. Maybe she was too perfect. All I knew while I danced with her was, there was no other place I wanted to be, even if God didn't want me to be. They were my two girls.

Over the next few years I continued my research on a very low-profile basis. It was not as fast as God intended, but at least I was making some progress. Abigail was growing up to be a wonderful daughter. We had lots of laughs together. At this point Jillian never gave me any more trouble or problems for me to doubt her again. I never heard her speak in that dark voice either. We got along very well until the sickness came. I was diagnosed with a rare disease that you hardly ever hear about. It is called celiac disease. This is a person's inability to consume gluten, which is in virtually everything. If left untreated this can cause heart failure and intestinal cancer. Like a fool I went untreated...

*Chapter Nine*

# Celiac Disease

It was Abigail's first day of kindergarten and the teacher had set up a meet-and-greet called "Our first tea party."

Abigail said, "Mommy, are you going to take me?"

Jillian said, "I won't be able to take you today. Mommy has to be at work right away so Daddy will have to take you."

Abigail put her head down and said, "All right, Mommy."

I said, "Are you all right, Abigail? Are you worried or embarrassed about Daddy going?"

Abigail nodded her head yes.

I said, "Try not to worry, sweetie. We will make the best of it as we always do."

Jillian said, "I need to go, please get back with me later about it and let me know how the tea party with her went."

Jillian collected her bag and her purse and walked out the front door. I reached down and picked up Abigail and set her down on the counter. Abigail sat there looking sad.

I said, "I know you were hoping that Mom would go, but we don't always get what we want in life. Today we need to make the best of the situation and go there with a good attitude and have a good time. Besides, you get your dad."

Abigail looked up at me and said, "That's right, my daddy. I just wanted Mommy to go because all the other mommies are going."

I said, "I understand it's a girl thing. But just so you know, dads enjoy tea also."

Abigail said, "I never see you drink tea, Daddy."

I said, "That's a great observation; okay, you got me there. So today's my first tea party. I am excited to go and meet your new teacher and friends."

Abigail said, "Aren't you even scared just a little?"

I said, "To be completely honest, I am more worried about you."

Abigail said, "I am okay, Daddy, please get me down now so we can go."

We drove to the school and parked the car. On our way inside, Abigail quickly noticed that she was the only one that brought her dad. When we arrived at the classroom door there stood Mrs. Hunter, her new kindergarten teacher.

Mrs. Hunter said, "Why hello there, I am Mrs. Hunter, your new kindergarten teacher; what is your name?"

Abigail smiled and said, "My name is Abigail Martin and this is my dad James."

I said, "It's nice to meet you, Mrs. Hunter."

Mrs. Hunter gave us some nametags and said, "It's very nice to meet you both. Please find a table to sit at."

I said, "Thank you."

We walked inside the classroom and we heard a familiar voice say, "Over here, Abigail. Please come and sit next to me."

It was her friend Clare from childcare and her mom. We had a great time meeting everyone and Abigail felt special because she had the only dad there that day. A half an hour later, Mrs. Hunter asked for all of the parents to leave. It was time for the children to be alone with Mrs. Hunter.

Abigail gave me a big hug and said, "I will be okay, Daddy. I will see you in a few hours."

I said, "I know you will. I'll see you soon. Have fun, sweetie."

Abigail walked away and I walked out into the hallway. I stood out there with all the other nervous parents watching their children. We all were trying not to cry. My baby girl was growing up.

One of the moms in the group began to cry and said, "I think what you did today was extraordinary. That baby girl will never forget this."

Another mom said, "I agree. You would never see my husband here. He never spends any time with the girls."

I said, "Thank you, I was honored to be here. The tea was pretty good."

Most of the moms giggled at my remark. I took one last look to check on Abigail. She was having a great time being with her friends. That night when Jillian came home, she asked Abigail how her first day at kindergarten went.

Abigail said, "Mrs. Hunter is really nice and I made new friends. Clare is in my class along with that silly boy Jacob."

Jillian said, "I think Jacob likes you. And when they do that's what boys do, they get silly."

Abigail said, "Boys are gross. I don't want anything to do with them. They smell funny too."

I started laughing along with Jillian. Abigail was so adorable. I had a great time teaching Abigail all about life. When she was six, she did pretty good learning how to ride a bike. She only wiped out a couple of times. When we went to church Abigail learned about Jesus. She almost had the same response as I did. Although she did not get up on the pew and express herself like I did, she shared her feelings with the priest after the service was over. Every day we spent together made us closer. Jillian and Abigail's relationship got further and further apart. Many times I tried to encourage Jillian to be a better parent by spending time with her. She always had an excuse for it. But she also made the most money and took care of us the best she knew how. I have to give her that credit. It was exciting to see Abigail experience life and learn from my mistakes I made as a child. She was as eager to learn and educate herself as I was. That made me even more proud of her. When Abigail turned 15 years old and wanted to start dating boys, I was not quite ready for that.

She surprised me one day by asking me if it was okay to date a boy from school. I was lying in the backyard in the hammock when she came back from a sleepover at her friend Clare's house.

Abigail said, "Dad, can we talk for a while?"

I said, "Of course we can... How are you? I did not hear you come home. How was the sleepover?"

Abigail said, "It was fun. We watched old scary movies. Then I couldn't sleep, my mind was filled with fear of something coming from inside of the closet or from under the bed."

I laughed a little and said, "I figured as much."

Abigail said, "Just about everyone at school has boyfriends. I was wondering if it was okay for me to date."

I sat there a second, surprised, and then looked up at her and said, "I think it's okay if you're responsible with it. Schoolwork is first."

Abigail took a deep breath and said, "Thank you, Dad! You are so easygoing and understanding. There is no way I could have asked Mom for this. She is so old school."

I said, "She may be old school but she cares about you deeply. She just worries that you might make the mistakes she made when she was young. I will tell her I said its okay for you to date."

Abigail said, "Thank you so much, Dad!"

I said, "No problem. I can't stop the birds and bees from getting together, it's part of nature. Speaking of birds and bees, did by chance Mom have the talk with you?"

Abigail turned a little red and said, "What talk… you mean about safe sex? All Mom does is talk at me, Dad. She is not like you at all. I can hear her now saying, 'get the dishwasher emptied,' 'clean your room,' 'why is the peanut butter out?' I was in the middle of making my sandwich…she is so weird, Dad. Besides it's cool, Dad, I have friends and we talk about it. We talk a lot!"

I said, "Abigail, I just want you to be safe and an adult about it. Your mom loves you even if she does weird stuff."

I stood up and gave her a hug and said, "Let's go eat some peanut butter off of a spoon."

Abigail said, "See, Dad, you're so easygoing and I know what condoms are."

As we walked to the house I said, "You are getting older and you're going to be an adult before too long. Let's get you an appointment with the doctor to talk about taking a pill as a precaution. Thanks for sharing that about condoms."

Abigail said, "How old were you the first time you had sex? Was it with Mom?"

I said, "To be completely honest it wasn't. I was young when I had sex for the first time."

Abigail said, "How old?"

I pulled out the jar of peanut butter. Abigail reached for two spoons and we sat down at the table in the kitchen.

I said, "I can't believe we are having this conversation, Abigail. I... was fourteen when I did... well you know."

Abigail said, "Wow, Dad, that is young. Who was the lucky girl?"

I said, "I can't share that with you. All I can say is that she was special and you should do the same thing. Wait until the time is right, okay?"

Abigail said, "I can respect that, Dad. It's not good to kiss and tell."

I said, "There is a time and place for that as well. You will know when...I think."

Abigail said, "I understand what you're trying to say."

I reached for more peanut butter with my spoon.

Abigail said, "Mom gets grossed out when we do that."

I said, "I know, just the other day she was lecturing me to be a better parent and to be a better example to you. I say if it's your own jar of peanut butter, enjoy! Who makes the peanut-butter rules anyways?"

Abigail giggled a little and stuck her spoon in the jar to get another scoop.

Abigail said, "It will be our secret, Dad. Please do not tell Mom about the boyfriend thing just yet please. Maybe I will talk with her on my own. I will have her take me to get the pill so you don't have to worry about it."

I said, "Whatever you want. Let me know if you need my help. I am not embarrassed to take you. Who do you think buys all of the female products in this house?"

Abigail stood up and put her spoon in the sink and began rinsing it off.

She turned around and said, "Oh Dad…thank you for listening to me. I am glad I can say what's on my mind to you without you judging me and getting angry with me."

I said, "That's what dads are for…I think?"

Abigail said, "Dad, I know you had a rough childhood. And I know you worry about if you're being a great dad all of the time... And just so you know, I think you're the best dad ever. Not only do I think that but my friends think so to. I mean you have been taking us to Cedar Point every summer and sometimes again in October during Holloweekends. What dad does that? I mean we talk all of the time. We go up north too. My friends' moms think you're hot and ask if you're single a lot. My friends are so jealous of what we have."

I said, "Thank you, sweetie, and get your homework done now if you can before dinner. We are going out when Mom comes home."

Abigail smiled and said, "I did it all in sixth period on Friday. Mr. Fillmore was gone and we had a sub. Mr. Fillmore forgot to leave instructions so the sub let us do whatever we wanted as long as we were quiet. So Clare and I did the rest of our homework."

I said, "You got to love that."

Abigail said, "It was great. Where are we going for dinner?"

I said, "Somewhere to get a big steak!"

The years went by fast and Abigail became a young woman practically overnight. I began to fulfill my promise to God and continued researching information and began to put the book together in my mind first. I must say I was doing quite well remembering all my notes. I got to a point where I could not trust anyone. Jillian had made me so paranoid of people. Jillian began to be very distant and did not want to help me overcome my disease. I couldn't understand why she acted the way she did. What I researched about celiac, I could not find a way to postpone it or cure it. No doctors could help me in any way. I got worse and worse to where hospice was the last call. As I lay in bed ill, Jillian began to tear through my things searching for something. I could barely speak, and when I did it was in a faint whisper.

After hearing all of the noise Abigail came into the room and said, "Mom, what are you doing?"

Jillian looked up at her and said, "Abigail, this is not your business; please leave!"

Abigail said, "But Mother, why are you doing this, especially while Dad is sick?"

Jillian pointed at the door and gave her an evil look. One I had only seen once before…the day I burnt my notes. Abigail looked back at me as she left; I winked at her. Abigail smiled as she disappeared around the corner. I knew I could only trust Abigail. After a couple of weeks of tearing up the house, Jillian finally came clean on what she was searching for. Jillian climbed on top of the bed and sat on me. She grabbed my shirt with both of her hands.

She tugged on my shirt and pulled me up from the bed, screaming, "Where is the book, you son of a bitch! I have been waiting all of these years!"

I did not say a word to her. I just stared into her eyes and watched as they turned black. Darkness quickly filled her veins.

In a deep dark voice Jillian said, "It's your last chance, God will not help you now! You have embarrassed him for too long! Trust me, I know firsthand!"

With all the energy I had I said, "It doesn't matter anymore. Do with me what you must, Lucifer."

Jillian slammed me down onto the bed and stood up next to me, furious.

As she slowly turned, I could see the veins in her head and neck turning darker and darker.

The veins in her arms turned black as she screamed, "I wasted all of these years being patient! I took care of you! I fucked you whenever you wanted! You owe me, James! I promised that book to Lucifer! He is going to kill me now if I don't return it to him!"

I remained quiet and continued staring at her.

Jillian leaned down next to me and said, "One last time…where is the book messenger!"

I was so ill I could not move or say anything. I could barely keep my eyes open to look at her. My mind began to race and my heart began to sing like never before!

"I told you so! Now on your deathbed will you listen?"

I figured that it was God rubbing it in. I wanted God to know I had kept my faith and my promise to him. I knew deep in my heart that he was right, but I went against his wishes. I guess now I'm going to pay the ultimate price: Death.

Jillian began to pack her bags. She felt if she left town she could run from Lucifer's wrath.

Jillian screamed, "Dammit, James, help me help you! Lucifer can heal you if you just give me the damn book! We can be together, don't you want that?"

I did nothing. I could only look at her with disgust.

Jillian yelled, "Dammit, James… We can be to-gether…don't you want that, James? Are you listening to me…are you just going to lie there and die?"

She continued packing. When she finished packing, I figured she was going to kill me or at least try. She came in after packing her car and walked through the house one last time. Abigail hid in her room with the door locked.

She came into the room and as calmly as she could say it she said, "James, for what it's worth you were the best thing that ever happened to me. Before I leave for good, I want you to know I sold my soul to have these looks and this fantastic body. I have known for years you wanted to know who I really am. Truth is I am from California like I said but I wanted out so badly. I looked like a small ugly troll like my mother. I begged God for help but help never arrived. I was ready to kill myself. When I went to go do it and was at the crossroads in my life, Lucifer showed up and promised to help me if I did him a favor in return. He asked me what I wanted. I asked for this body and great looks. Just a flick of his finger, he made it happen. I was so happy and eager to please him, I asked what he wanted. All Lucifer wanted was the book. The book that would change the world, he called it. He told me all about you. So he brought me to Michigan and set me up with a job and money. He knew when you slept, ate, and worked most of the time. Lucifer owns me now. I know I won't ever see you again, and I want you to know that I really did love you for who you were. If I got the book from you, I was going to continue to stay with you. That was our final arrangement."

Jillian kissed my lips and walked to the door and slowly turned around.

She looked back at me and said, "I love you so much!"

She walked away. I could hear the car start and I listened as she drove away. Abigail came in the room crying after she heard her mom leave the house.

Abigail said, "I heard the whole thing, Dad, and I am sorry. Mom knows the devil, seriously? Is there anything I can do to help you?"

I went to speak but couldn't. I began to get angry. I couldn't believe Jillian worked for the devil. I felt like a dumb-ass. I thought maybe a possession at most. She'd actually sold her soul to help him.

With all the energy I had I said, "Pray for me. Tell God I am sorry."

Abigail got down on her knees and began to pray to God for forgiveness on my behalf.

Abigail said, "God, please forgive my father for he has sinned in the worst way. I know I'm asking a lot of you. God, if you can hear me please forgive him. He is my dad and he did the best he could. I need him, I love him, God, please! It was not his fault he was being tricked by the devil!"

Abigail began to cry and reached up and grabbed my hand, begging God for his help.

She said, "God, please listen to me once. Please help my father get well and he will finish the book as promised. I am not sure what it is but I will help him, please forgive him!"

Abigail looked at me and squeezed my hand real tight.

Abigail said, "He will start on it as soon as he is healed. I will make him quit his job and take away his car keys, please, God! Please!"

Abigail stood up and hugged me tight.

She whispered, "Dad, that is all I can do for you. The doctors can't help you either. Please pray for yourself and confess your sins right now!"

Abigail continued to cry. I could feel her tears drop onto my face and run down to my ear.

I closed my eyes and for the first time in years I said, "God, I confess my sins. I should've listened to you in the first place. Why didn't you tell me the truth about Jillian? If you knew she was the devil's advocate, why did you put me through this all of these years? God, are you there?"

God did not answer. I opened my eyes for a moment and Abigail was still crying, holding my hand. She appeared to be praying on my behalf again.

I whispered, "Abigail, I love you. It's okay now."

With the rest of my remaining energy I said, "It's my fault."

I passed out. I went into a deep sleep for days. When I woke up Abigail was there taking care of me. She had called her grandma for help.

I could hear my mom say, "James, it's about time you woke up."

It was not long for me. I took a look around the room and then passed back out. I fell into a deep sleep. When I did God was there.

God said, "James, I heard your confession and Abigail's prayers. That girl loves her daddy!"

I said, "Yes she does."

God said, "Do you feel you have enough knowledge now to write my book?"

I said, "I do, God, I have continued my research since we spoke last. I have much of the book written in my mind. The only thing left to work out is the coded message you wanted."

God said, "You sacrificed a great deal of your life for that woman and child. You have put mankind at even a greater risk."

I said, "I'm sorry, God, please forgive me. I do not know what else to say except, love is blind."

God said, "Yes it is. I admire your courage for standing up to me. But you ignored my request and me; this is why I made you ill. I gave you celiac disease because there is no known cure for it once it's out of control. I did not want you to die, but I did not want man's medicine to cure you. I will heal you, James, with the condition that you start my book immediately. I will give you the security you need to finish. I want you to quit your job and remain at home until the book is finished. Send Abigail or your mother for food or refreshments. You will contact me immediately after you are finished. Do you clearly understand me?"

I said, "I do. Thank you, God, and I really am sorry for not listening to you and especially my heart."

God said, "What is done is done. You learn from

it and you move on. You will begin to feel better in a few days."

I said, "Abigail would want me to thank you too."

God said, "I will tell her myself and in my own way."

I said, "Okay."

A few days later, I began to feel better and was able to get up and walk a little. It felt good to go to the bathroom instead of making a mess of myself. My mother became even more of a better person after watching me go through the disease. I think my situation restored her and my stepdad's faith because they talked about going back to church. I began my work on the book and continued my research for odds and ends. God came to me again weeks later. I had so many questions for him; things were not quite clear to me.

God said, "James, how are you feeling now?"

I said, "God, I feel excellent. I began the book and things are looking great."

God said, "That is good to hear."

I said, "God, I have a question or two if you could help?"

God said, "Please ask."

I said, "God, who was the angel that helped my whole life? Things happened to me that should have been my end."

God said, "Well now; there were many. But the one in charge was Gabrielle. Gabrielle is my general.

He oversees many things on my behalf."

I said, "God, could I meet him someday?"

God went silent for a moment and said, "Well he has been here the whole time watching you. It's all right, Gabrielle, go ahead."

Gabrielle appeared just like that. He startled me. He was so tall and handsome. His wings were so large and white.

I stood up and stuck out my hand and said, "Thank you for watching out for me."

Gabrielle's wings folded up as he said, "I was honored!"

Gabrielle reached forward and shook my hand. He placed his hand on my shoulder and then slowly pushed me down to my chair.

Gabrielle said, "James, you have kept me busy for a while now. Ever since you were a little boy I have been by your side."

I said, "I wish we could have met sooner."

Gabrielle said, "James, it does not work that way. The only reason I show my face now is you are a part of me and with God's permission. You are like a brother. A little one, I might add! Ha! Ha! I remember the first time God sent me to look over you. You were four years old with curly hair."

## Chapter Ten

# The Explanation

Gabrielle continued, "You just received Shane as a puppy. I laughed at the way you two played together. You were inseparable."

I said, "I remember. I miss Shane deeply."

Gabrielle said, "I know you do. Shane was sent to look after you while I was away. He was my eyes and ears."

I began to cry at the thought. I loved him like a brother. I remembered him always getting off of the large chain and appearing out of thin air.

Gabrielle said, "I was so proud of you that day at your grandma's when Shane was dying. You honored him well by fighting for him."

I said, "I was so mad that day at my mom. I knew Shane was dying but I loved him and did not want him to go. Shane had that stupid hip disease and could no longer walk. He was lying out on the patio when the animal-control police came. I had a hammer in my hand from building my fort when they pulled in the driveway. I ran to Shane's side and put his head on my lap to comfort him. When the officers came to get him, anger like I never felt before came over me to protect him."

Gabrielle smiled. I continued to cry. It was like I was there at that very moment.

I said, "When the officer reached for Shane I swung the hammer at him, causing him to jump back."

The officer says, "Whoa now, kid, take it easy!"

As I watched him and waited for him to make his next move, my mom and grandma came out and grabbed me from behind. I fought so hard to get them off of me. The officer quickly gave Shane a shot and put him to sleep forever.

I yelled at the top of my lungs, "NOOOOOO!"

My grandma said they were so sorry. But it had to be done. He was suffering! I hated them for doing that to Shane for a long time. As I got a little older I realized it was part of the life cycle.

Gabrielle said, "James, you have been through many tragic events. You have done well to overcome them and adapt. That's life!"

I said, "Thank you."

Gabrielle said, "Shane was a great angel, but his time was up as it will be for everyone on earth. I hope you realize this."

I said, "I do. It makes me appreciate life that much more. What a gift."

Gabrielle sat there a minute and said, "Do you

remember the car that hit you when you were a little boy?"

I closed my eyes and said, "I do just like it just
had happened."

Gabrielle said, "I was walking behind you when
you turned to avoid hitting that puppy. You went in
between the parked cars and into the street. As the
car came, I flew as fast as I could and wrapped myself
around you at the time of impact. That car had some
force, didn't it?"

I said, "It sure did. I couldn't believe I was alive."

Gabrielle said, "We flew over twenty feet and
I landed us safely on the lawn; do you remember
the neighbor woman? She has a set of pipes on her,
doesn't she?"

I said, "Yes, like it just happened."

Gabrielle said, "James, I am sorry for not being
there when the rock hit you and the apple incident. Both
of those times I was away helping on tragic events."

God came to the rescue on those.

God said, "James, you did keep me on my toes a
few times. I stayed with you all night to make sure you
did not have a concussion. Your mother was so worried
about you. Little Mike prayed for you until he fell asleep.
Do you remember the wagon jump at Grandma's?"

I said, "I will never forget. That was pretty cool."

God said, "When you went down the second time,

I could not help myself but to eject you two like that."

God laughed a little.

Gabrielle said, "I wish I could have seen that."

God said, "It was priceless! You two splashed into the water like a couple of pebbles."

I laughed with them.

God said, "When you got to the top of the hill to dry off, you looked like two wet Saint Bernards. Do you remember the wind?"

I said, "I do. As it began to blow I told Mike to hold his arms out so we could pretend to fly away."

God said, "I was drying you off, James."

I said, "Oh! I didn't know."

Gabrielle said, "The wheelbarrow ride was not funny! You could have killed yourself, James."

God said, "Getting Grandma upset like that was not good either."

I said, "I was trying to have fun?"

Gabrielle said, "Well it was fun the second time. I showed Jason who was boss when you hung on through the turns."

I smiled because I knew then I was not strong enough to hold on.

Gabrielle said, "On the fourth turn God told me enough and I slid you off, sliding you up to the tree. I am the one that punctured a hole in it and folded the barrel up so you could not use it anymore."

I said, "That was too bad, that was a lot of fun."

God said, "There is nothing wrong with having fun, just do not kill yourself doing it."

I smiled at Gabrielle and said, "I am sorry."

God said, "Lucifer has made many attempts on your life. Gabrielle has done a wonderful job keeping him at bay!"

Gabrielle said, "Especially when the car hit you and Samantha. I was in the backseat when the car struck us. I quickly wrapped you both up in my wings, accidentally causing you two to bump heads. Remember?"

I said, "I do."

God said, "Let's not forget the bike jump, and the time at the farm?"

Gabrielle said, "I can't take credit for the farm incident. That was all Chantelle. The bike landing though was cool, huh?"

I said, "It was. So did my Uncle Dean. He thought it was a miracle."

I sat there for a brief second and then said, "Chantelle was awesome!"

God said, "She is."

Gabrielle raised his eyebrows at me and smiled. I smiled back.

God said, "That's enough, you two."

Gabrielle said, "James, I was impressed when you jumped the curb that day in Jerry's car. You made

Lucifer very angry! I loved it!"

I said, "That was a strange day. I did not want to lie to Jerry about that."

God said, "Do not worry about him, he is fine. You needed to learn what premonitions are and to trust them. You did and I was proud of you for that.

There have been many incidents in your life, James, that we were there and we were not. Like your father turning to evil."

God paused for a moment and then said, "As far as the sinners, I can only help the spirits that earned their way back."

I said, "God, I realize this now. I will share it with the world as well."

God said, "I have a new mission for you if you think you are ready?"

Gabrielle said, "I think he is. He has enough training to help us. He survived the Jillian situation. He honored his doing with Jillian and raised his daughter."

God said, "James, after you finish my book I want to offer you a chance of a lifetime!"

Gabrielle said, "If I may say, sir, could I have him in my legion?"

God said, "Let's see what James has to say first, Gabrielle. James, when you are done with the book and you feel your life is complete, I want to offer you a chance to be an angel. I feel you have earned it. I love the way you love the earth and mankind. As the population grows we have more to do."

I sat there looking at Gabrielle and the smile on his face. He looked so excited for me.

Gabrielle said, "Say yes, fool!"

I stood up and said, "I would be honored!"

Gabrielle said, "Very well then, I will make the arrangements. How long before the book is complete—a week? a month? I need to get you through angel camp training!"

I said, "I will go as quickly as I can and keep you posted."

Gabrielle said, "Very well."

God said, "James, I am proud of you."

I said, "I am grateful for the opportunity."

God said, "We will go and let you get finished."

Gabrielle said, "James, I am excited for you! I will be here if you need me! Just ask!"

## Chapter Eleven

# God's Message

The truth is, you've read *most* of the message. The remaining coded message God wanted you to read is at the end of this book. The message started at the beginning of this book with a journey of a young boy chosen by God. His journey was a very rough one at times, and a wonderful one at times too. That's life! It's not perfect. It's full of change and hate and anger and jealousy and the list goes on. It was not in any code at all. It was in plain English. See, all God wants is for us to enjoy the earth and for us to quit blowing it up.

Get rid of the cities of sin and for us to teach our children the rules. Be parents to them, not their best friend or bff! If you cannot be a parent, then step down so someone can. We need to bring back the **Declaration of Independence** and follow the Ten Commandments better. I think if we all try a little harder, it would not take much at all. I believe in you!!! Let's do it in baby steps together. I think the first thing that needs to go is nuclear weapons. Then, you decide what's next.

If it were I, I think it's time to join one another and repair the earth. I know each and every one of us does have an important role in life. Have the courage to follow your heart; it's singing to you. Are you listening? Join hands and do away with your differences. Guide and educate your children to make the Earth a better place for everyone to complete their journey of life. Remember, you are only here once and you need to make the best of it. I feel choosing good over evil is best for us all. All of us need to continue our education. Remember where we came from so we know where we are headed.

I will say it again! Remember to do away with the cities of sin and teach your children to follow in your footsteps so they can teach their children. Take responsibility for your own actions. Read and follow the Ten Commandments. Invest in your church. When the earth is in harmony, I think the storms will be gone. When the balance of life is achieved, you will all be rewarded with a great life for your children and their children. I feel everyone should apply these words to their lives, health, respect, honor, trust, and communication. I think you would be rewarded with a guilt-free life. God asked me to be short and to the point with the coded message. He did not want you to spend the whole day searching for it. But it must be earned!

This is how the code cipher works. 1-2-3. Column 1 represents the page number. Column 2 represents the line. Column 3 represents the character including spaces and all characters. I am off to angel training now! Remember... God's watching!!!

63-3-13 51-6-28

16-2-24 8-5-17 34-10-44

217-2-3 7-3-18 67-13-12 45-4-23 169-13-2 16-8-5 22-4-10

39-15-20 33-3-9 52-7-26

53-4-5 75-24-4 40-6-6

85-5-10 83-15-22

81-4-10 73-4-36 34-4-3

30-7-21 6-7-21 13-4-4 58-11-28 85-8-3 64-4-12

24-5-11 22-7-38

7-3-14 15-7-5 25-5-17

6-7-6 8-8-30

27-2-1 40-5-3 10-3-11 55-5-3 10-8-5

43-10-20 50-7-15 14-10-5

80-3-14 34-4-14

66-3-53 22-7-12 51-3-11 87-3-3 55-4-13

12-12-21

28-9-7 8-8-5 68-12-6

If you are in a hurry and do not wish to search for it and earn it, turn to the last page for the answer.

*To all mankind:*

*Get rid of the cities of sin or learn how to swim.*

*12-12-21*

*GOD*

CPSIA information can be obtained at www.ICGtesting.com
Printed in the USA
BVOW03s1226061114

373976BV00026B/388/P

9 781478 742203